She felt a surge of sexual heat so strong she caught her breath...

Max rose, never letting his gaze drop, and Claire felt powerless herself to break the connection.

Closer.

Never breaking stride until he stood right up in front of her, so close she could see the stubble on his face and glimpse the black flecks in his dark brown eyes. Eyes that stared at her with an intensity that made her shiver.

He moved even closer. She didn't step back but held her ground, held his gaze.

He grabbed her shoulders, pulled her to him and kissed her with the same urgency he'd drunk deep of the stream only moments ago.

She felt the roughness of a face that hadn't seen a razor in two days, the coldness of the river water on his lips, the hot, potent energy of the man flowing through him and into her.

She wanted more.

More of that energy, more of his solid sexiness in her arms.

And more of the feeling that something positive and wonderful was happening in the midst of this madness....

Dear Reader,

In *Breakaway,* book two in the Last Bachelor Standing trilogy, aeronautics billionaire Max Varo is looking for a challenge. He finds it in Alaska with sexy bush pilot Claire Lundstrom. Max and Claire also love playing hockey and it was great fun watching them challenge each other on the ice and off.

A thirty-five-year-old bachelor, Max is a little tired of being courted for his wealth. Going undercover for his company to see what's up with Polar Air, the small airline owned by Claire and her grandmother, is supposed to be a lark, not change his whole life. For Claire, having an affair with the newest bush pilot is only supposed to be a lark. Not change her whole life. It's funny how love can mess up a perfectly good plan.

An avid hiker myself, I based Polar Air on some of the small airlines I've flown with to get into remote hiking areas. And the bear encounter? That's based on my own experiences.

Up next? Look for bachelor number three Dylan's story, *Final Score,* coming in June 2014.

Visit me on the web at www.nancywarren.net.

Happy reading!

Nancy Warren

Nancy Warren

Breakaway

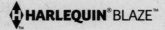

HARLEQUIN® BLAZE™

Recycling programs
for this product may
not exist in your area.

ISBN-13: 978-0-373-79797-4

BREAKAWAY

Copyright © 2014 by Nancy Warren

www.Harlequin.com

Printed in U.S.A.

ABOUT THE AUTHOR

USA TODAY bestselling author Nancy Warren lives in the Pacific Northwest, where her hobbies include skiing, hiking and snowshoeing. She's an author of more than thirty novels and novellas for Harlequin and has won numerous awards. Visit her website at www.nancywarren.net for news on upcoming titles.

Books by Nancy Warren

HARLEQUIN BLAZE

*Last Bachelor Standing

HARLEQUIN COSMO RED-HOT READS

HER VALENTINE FANTASY

Other titles by this author available in ebook format.

To get the inside scoop on Harlequin Blaze and its talented writers, be sure to check out blazeauthors.com.

I dedicate this book to Sharon and Stewart McKenzie

for their many years of friendship and career help.

I love you guys.

Acknowledgments:

I have come to rely on friends, friends of friends, and in this book, husbands and sons of friends who are so generous in spilling about things they know. Thanks to Mary, Trish and Ted for their assistance in flying and crashing a plane. Thanks to Karen, her son Guillaume and his friend Leo for brilliantly helping with the big hockey scene. Thanks to John for all his wilderness backpacking expertise. I dedicate this book to all of you, with thanks.

1

THREE MEN SAT around a campfire on a warm June evening at a wilderness site in Oregon. All were rugged, fit and experienced outdoorsmen. Two were single. One was about to be married. Four days of kayaking had seemed like the perfect choice for their last trip as three single guys. Max Varo, Adam Shawnigan and Dylan Cross had known each other since they started playing together in the sandbox three decades earlier. Now in their mid-thirties, they had successful careers and still played together, though now their sandbox was a hockey rink.

The fire crackled, throwing a little light and a little warmth their way. Max's muscles ached from paddling all day against choppy currents. He rolled his shoulders, knowing tomorrow would bring more of the same. Their dinner, beef Stroganoff that came in a foil pack from someplace called Backpackers' Pantry, had been eaten. Now they sat around holding metal mugs of campfire coffee, their tents pitched behind them, kayaks pulled up for the night. Max and Adam stared into the fire, each lost in his own thoughts, while Dylan, always the restless one, built an inuksuk out of nearby stones. Then, bored with that, he suddenly said, "So, Adam, any regrets about getting hitched?"

Adam turned from the fire to glance over at his old friend. "No," he said simply. "In fact, if I could be granted one wish, it would be to have met Serena earlier."

Recalling some of the women Adam had dated in his very full bachelor life, Max was inclined to wish the same thing. He'd been forced to spend time with some of Adam's women and they tended to be—well, flaky would be putting it kindly. But Serena Long had been right for Adam from the first day they'd met. Not that either of them had known that, of course.

Max took some pride in the fact that he'd been the one to introduce his old friend, a performance coach, to his buddy, a cop who was having some performance issues in the hockey arena. When Serena started getting threatening emails, Adam had done everything he could to keep her safe, even as the crazy psycho who was stalking her stepped up the threats. But some good had come out of it. A notorious killer was behind bars, and Adam and Serena were getting married.

"One wish. Wow," Dylan said. "Hey, Max, if you could have one wish what would it be?"

As he opened his mouth Dylan held up a hand. "And no 'world peace' or 'cure cancer' allowed. Let's hope we'd all man up and choose something noble if we actually stumbled across some genie who could give us anything. But, you know, what would you want for yourself?"

Max hoped he'd be big enough to ask for world peace if this magic genie appeared, but he suspected he was too weak. There was one thing that all the money and hard work in the world couldn't buy. "I'd ask for infection-proof ears. Retroactive to childhood."

There weren't many people in the world who knew

his secret regret, but these two guys were the closest friends he had. They knew that he'd always dreamed of being an astronaut. And that a couple of stupid childhood ear infections had weakened his ears to the point that he was out of the running before he even started. By the time he finished high school he knew he'd never be an astronaut.

"Yeah, that really sucked. But, you know, how many people get to be astronauts? For real?"

"I would have made it," he said with the simple certainty of a man who had the tenacity to set his sights on a goal and pursue it single-mindedly. He had the smarts and the right temperament. What he didn't have were the ears. He'd been ridiculously successful at everything he'd set his mind to. Except his dream.

"Life didn't turn out too bad for you," Adam said. "I bet most astronauts would trade their jobs for the billions you're worth."

Max shrugged. "I'd take the trade."

"Yeah, I know."

Money was easy to make in Max's experience. Even though he couldn't take part in space missions he'd studied astrophysics and invented a climate-control system that was eventually purchased by NASA. He'd refined his system and licensed it to most of the world's major airlines. Obscenely rich at thirty-five, he now spent his time working as a venture capitalist. Money wasn't the problem. If he had a problem, he suspected that it was boredom.

"Bought any companies lately?" Dylan asked.

"As a matter of fact, I am thinking of buying an airline."

"I hope it's a big American one because I have to tell you, last time I flew—"

"Nope. It's called Polar Air."

"Polar Air? Are you kidding me? Sounds like an air-conditioning system."

"Well, it's an airline. A small outfit that operates in Alaska."

"If I had your money I'd buy yachts. And really big jewelry for bathing-suit models." Dylan shook his head. "You buy Bush League air."

"And that's why he's rich and you're not," Adam said.

"What about you, smart-ass?" Max said to Dylan. "What would you have if you were granted one wish? And no world peace for you, either."

"Or Max's billions."

Dylan grinned, his teeth gleaming white in the fire-light. He thought for a moment then grew serious. "I'd choose a superpower, obviously. Superstrength? X-ray vision? I can never decide."

"Come on, dude. Quit messing around."

Adam said, "You know, I think he's being serious."

"Bet your ass I am."

Max shook his head and asked Adam, "Why are we friends with this guy?"

"Comic relief?" Adam tipped his head to the side and caught the coffee cup that came flying toward him. Having a serious conversation with Dylan was like talking physics with a golden retriever.

Dylan stood, stretched his arms high. "Well, one thing is for sure, I'm still in the running for Last Bach-elor Standing and the odds are getting shorter."

Max laughed. "It's down to you and me now, buddy. And I play to win."

MAX RETURNED TO his office in Hunter, Washington, after his long weekend of kayaking and found that, as usual, everything was running smoothly. His staff looked happy to see him, but it wasn't like there was a lineup of people needing his input.

He was smart enough to hire the best people he could find to work for him. He gave them autonomy, paid them well and was generous in praise and bonuses. As a result, his staff members were loyal, hardworking and proactive. His business ran like clockwork, his wealth grew exponentially every day.

Varo Enterprises was so successful it even had an entire division devoted to funding charities and worthy causes.

And Maximilian Varo, CEO of Varo Enterprises, was bored.

After a meeting with his key people at which he mostly agreed with their suggestions and approved decisions and expenditures, he asked Leslie Adamson, the manager he'd put in charge of the Polar Air acquisition, how it was going. Leslie pulled out the relevant file. "It's going all right. It's a pretty small deal by our standards. Shouldn't be any problem buying for the right price and then putting in some good people to turn it around." She flipped back a few pages in the file. "Polar Air used to be a successful regional airline. Started in the '50s with a couple of bush pilots, husband and wife. Lynette and Carl Lundstrom.

"They flew supplies to hunting and fishing lodges, carried mail, flew equipment to logging and mining operations. Got bigger, and more successful. They flew hikers, hunters, geologists, kayakers all over Alaska. Then in the last five years things have gone south. The recession had an impact, but they are way behind on payments to suppliers and they aren't keeping up with the times. We think there's plenty of business that they aren't going after. The fleet's in good shape, there's a small but loyal customer base. Could be a turnaround candidate to flip or we could keep it, maybe look at further acquisitions, expand as a regional airline."

He knew all about the financials of Polar Air. Max never bought a business he didn't understand and believe in. The small airline had some troubles, but the equipment was good, the pilots well trained. "You're right. The airline should be more successful."

Leslie nodded. "I don't like not knowing what the problems really are. What we need is somebody on the ground."

"Or in the air," he said.

Leslie agreed. "They've got an opening for a pilot. Somebody with a commercial pilot's license and some smarts could find out what's going on from inside the operation."

Some of his boredom began to lift. "You think we could get somebody in there?"

"My contact would definitely put in a good word with the management of Polar Air if we had a pilot. Sure."

"Then do it. I know just the person."

Max had learned to fly in high school, working construction in the summers so he could afford lessons. He'd trained for his commercial pilot's license a decade later. Even though his life had taken a different turn, he kept his license current. He owned a Cessna and an Otter and flew at every opportunity. He didn't have a ton of hours logged in Alaska but he had plenty logged in Washington and Oregon and he figured that had to count.

He was sure that Leslie would make it happen. She was that good.

She didn't even question his suitability for the bush-pilot job because she knew that he was also that good.

Max was about to do the thing he loved best. He was going to fly.

CLAIRE LUNDSTROM FLEW the Beaver floatplane over Spruce Bay, cruising along with the air currents. Her passengers, a father and son from Tennessee, were headed for Takwalnot, a wilderness fishing lodge, for a week. The dad, Don Carpenter, sat in the back, eyes glued to the rattling window. His son, Kyle, sat beside her in the front seat. He was eighteen and trying to be cool, but she could tell it was a thrill for him to be flying beside the pilot, enjoying an aerial view of some of the most spectacular scenery in the world. All three of them were linked by headsets.

"You picked a great day to fly," she said, enjoying the sunshine as much, or more, than her passengers. "That's Mount McKinley in the distance," she said. It was magnificent, snow-capped and majestic. She glanced down. Smiled. "Look to your left," she said. "See the whales?"

She dropped the plane lower, took a pass over a pod of grays breaching and playing in the water. Sun sparkled off a dorsal fin and one of the whales surfaced, blowing a plume of mist into the air. "Look," cried Kyle. "You can see the whole body under the water." Cameras came out and father and son had a moment of bonding. She imagined that was the point of the trip.

She never got tired of this. Of sharing the place she loved with those who came to visit. She turned and took another pass so her clients could enjoy watching the whales at play, banked the plane so Don could get a clearer photo. Then she turned and headed for the lodge.

"You're a fine pilot, ma'am, thank you," Don Carpenter said as she unloaded their fishing gear onto the dock.

"You're welcome."

"You seem too young to be flying planes."

She laughed. It wasn't the first time she'd heard such a comment. "My grandparents started Polar Air. I've been flying since I was sixteen years old." She didn't bother telling the Carpenters the sad part of her history. That her parents had been killed in a car crash coming home from a dinner party one night. Nobody's fault. The car had gone into a turn and skidded off a cliff thanks to a deadly combination of ice, poor visibility and old snow tires. Fifteen and grieving, she'd been sent to live with her grandparents. She'd planned on hating Spruce Bay and running away. But a lot of love, good food and time had helped ease her hurt. And when she was sixteen her grandfather put her in the copilot's seat and gave her the controls for a few amazing minutes.

From that moment she'd known what she wanted to do with her life.

She wasn't sixteen anymore. She was nearly thirty. And she still loved flying more than anything else she could think of.

Once she'd finished unloading the Carpenters and their baggage, three businessmen from Albuquerque were waiting for their return trip. She loaded them onto the plane, then assessed the trio. Some sunburns and a general air of satisfaction told her their week had gone well. "How was your trip?" she asked.

"Fantastic. We caught some of the nicest sockeye I've ever tasted."

For the price she knew they were paying for their week, she was glad they'd caught some salmon. Meant they'd tell their friends, maybe come back. "You'll never get better fishing than up here," she said into her headset.

Even the whales cooperated with her tour guide routine, hanging around in the same area where she'd last seen them. Once more she dipped down low, giving the men an up-close view of whales at play.

When she landed at the dock of Polar Air, she powered down and took a moment to enjoy the silence, before hopping down from the plane and tying up to the dock.

She had a couple of hours before her next flight, so she headed up the dock and turned, not to the office, but in the direction of her grandmother's house.

Lynette Lundstrom was nearing seventy-three and Claire's favorite person in the world. She usually found time to visit her grandmother every day, either for coffee or a sandwich. They ate dinner together at least twice a week.

She banged open the front door and headed for the kitchen, cheerfully calling out, "Coffee on?" She didn't immediately get a response.

She quickened her step and found her grandmother sitting at the big oak kitchen table with a scatter of papers fanned in front of her.

She pulled up a chair and sat down opposite her grandmother, concern building when she saw the expression on Lynette's face. "What's up?"

Lynette looked up at her, looking like an old woman for the first time Claire could remember. "I think we're in trouble. The bank is threatening to call in the mortgage."

Claire glanced at the fan of papers on the table. "What mortgage?"

The older woman was obviously upset. Her voice wavered. "Your grandfather and I started that airline back in the '50s," she reminded Claire as though she could possibly have forgotten the family history. "We used to fly in supplies for miners, fly in timber cruisers and transport Indian chiefs. We've helped with rescue missions. We delivered mail." She tapped her fingers angrily against the table. "My whole life is here and connected to Polar Air. How can a bank take this airline away?"

"Calm down, Grandma. Nobody's going to take our airline away from us. I don't think they can." She swallowed. "Can they?"

"The trouble is I've let things go a little. I know there have been some problems, but—"

"What problems?" Everything seemed fine to Claire. But she was busy with flights, and didn't have a lot of patience for paperwork and administration. Some of their previous business had dropped off, it was true, but they'd added a lot of new business through tourism.

Claire frowned over the sheets of paper Lynette passed to her. "Why didn't you tell me?" She glanced up at her grandmother's worried face.

"I didn't want to bother you. You're busy flying. Now that I don't fly anymore, I feel that I should at least be able to run the place. I thought business would pick up and we'd be able to pay the mortgages back."

Lynette turned to gaze out over a pair of old armchairs that sat by the window of her log house. The window faced one of the most spectacular views in Alaska. Probably the entire world. Set on a bluff overlooking the ocean, the house commanded views of crashing waves, of the islands out in the strait, and of the otters, whales, dolphins and seals that called the area home.

And they weren't the only ones. Lynette had called Spruce Bay home her whole life. Claire realized she'd been doing the same for almost half of hers.

"I didn't want to worry you," Lynette said once more.

"Well, I'm worried now. What's going on?"

"After your grandfather died, I left Frank in charge of day-to-day operations. They won't let me fly anymore and I'm not good in the office."

"I know." Lynette had been a bush pilot for forty years. It had nearly killed her when she'd had to give up her license after a mild heart attack. The irony was that the heart trouble hadn't slowed her grandmother down at all. It was losing her license that had devastated her. Fortunately, she'd found a new calling coaching the women's hockey team in Spruce Bay. It was something she'd done back when Claire first turned in her figure skates for a pair of speed skates.

Sometimes Claire felt guilty that she hadn't stepped in to run the airline after her grandfather died, but she loved to fly and she had no interest in running an airline. Like Lynette, she'd believed Frank Carmondy was both capable and honest.

"Oh, honey, I'm not sure. Frank came to me around five years ago and said we needed to get a bigger credit line. You know, we always used to have one. The recession was on and we needed to access some capital. He arranged it all and I signed the papers."

"Grandma," she said, making an effort to keep her voice calm, "how much money are we talking? And why the hell is the bank calling the loan?"

2

MAX LOVED TO FLY almost as much as he loved sex. In some ways the two were similar. The freedom, the feeling of utter contentment. The ride was sometimes wild, sometimes smooth and familiar but he always, always ended up with a thrill.

Today was no different. He flew over majestic stands of evergreens, interspersed with logging clear-cuts as he skirted the coast. His flight plan took him over tankers and cruise ships, a pod of hunting orcas. He landed his Cessna at Polar Air's airfield in Spruce Bay, and coasted until he came to a stop on a serviceable strip.

He turned off the engine, took off his headset. Climbed out of the plane and grabbed his battered briefcase.

He secured his plane and then entered the small, squat building that housed Polar Air.

And walked right into a very interesting situation.

The first thing he noted was the shapeliest backside he had ever seen. The rounded hips belonged to a dark-haired woman with a ponytail hanging down her back who was currently asking a portly middle-aged man in a Polar Air jacket some very pointed questions.

They were so deep in conversation that neither of

them had heard his entrance. He was about to cough or announce himself in some way, when she said, "I spent the last couple of hours looking at the financial records on the computer. It seems to me that this company's financial situation is worse than it should be." Max bit back his fake cough and listened. Seemed his flight up here was already paying off.

An ugly look came over the face of the guy at the desk. "What right do you have to study the books?"

"My grandmother asked me to."

"And you're an accountant now?"

"I've got eyes and a brain, Frank. I don't like what I discovered."

A deep flush began to mottle his ugly face. "What are you suggesting?"

"I'm suggesting," she said in a cool, even tone that was steel all the way through, "that the numbers aren't adding up."

"You and your grandmother would be lost without me. I think you'd better watch your tone, young lady."

"Where's the money, Frank?"

"I'm not listening to this, Claire. I'll call my lawyer if you don't shut up."

There was a beat of charged silence.

"I think that's a good idea. You should definitely call a lawyer. You're fired," she said.

Max didn't like the expression in the fat man's eyes. He didn't like the way he rose from his chair so he could loom over the woman. "You can't fire me."

"Yes. I can. And I just did. I think you'd better leave."

"You little bitch." The guy moved an inch closer to her and she didn't budge. "You can't make—"

Max decided it was time to make his presence felt.

"I think you were asked to leave," he said pleasantly, walking slowly toward the desk.

Both of the combatants turned to face him. He got his first glimpse of the front of the woman with the great ass. As he'd hoped, her front was as alluring—more so—than her back.

She might only stand as tall as his chin but she packed a lot of authority into her curvy body. He liked the way she filled out her jeans and the flight jacket that featured the Polar Air logo.

She'd fed her ponytail through a Polar Air ball cap and she wore sturdy boots.

No rings, he noted absently. In fact, the only jewelry she wore were small gold hoops in her earlobes. Her hazel eyes were big and round, with flecks of green and gold that fascinated him as he drew closer.

She didn't look thrilled at his interference, so he turned his attention to the fat guy who looked even less thrilled.

"Let me get the door for you."

Max wasn't a big man, but he was fit and tough. He took in the measure of the guy who'd been fired and decided he wasn't going to end up engaging in a barbarian fistfight. This guy was all blubber and bluster. Still, he kept his muscles on alert, stayed light on the balls of his feet in case he was wrong.

The man sneered at him. And at the woman. "This isn't over. You'll be hearing from my lawyer."

"Good," she said.

The guy shoved Max's shoulder on his way out and then slammed the door.

The slam was still echoing when he turned back to face the pretty woman. She didn't thank him for his assistance. Instead she said, "I was handling that. I didn't need your help."

"I know you didn't," he said reasonably. "But look at it from my point of view. Once I'd walked in and heard him threaten you, what was I going to do? Creep outside? You'd think I was a coward."

He saw her lips twitch as she tried to hold back a smile. "I'm Claire Lundstrom," she said. "How can I help you?"

"Max Varo," he said, holding out his hand. "I'm a pilot. Heard there was a job."

"Do you have an interview?"

"I did, but I think the guy I was interviewing with just got fired."

CLAIRE LIKED THE look of Max Varo. Nice-looking guy, she noted. Neatly trimmed dark hair, Latino, even features. Great body. His jeans and navy fleece couldn't hide a muscular build. He wasn't much taller than she was, but the package was nice. Sexy. He had big brown eyes with ridiculously thick, curly eyelashes that most women would kill for. They didn't make him look feminine, though. Simply added to the impact of those eyes.

She didn't know how loyal the dozen existing Polar Air pilots were to Frank, but she thought it would be good to have at least one pilot who was a new hire.

Even though she hadn't appreciated him butting in to go all Sir Galahad on her, she understood that his behavior showed courage and a sense of justice.

"Come into the back office and sit down," she said, leading him to a small room behind the main counter.

He settled himself in the vinyl visitor's chair and pulled out a résumé.

She scanned it quickly. "You've got all the right certifications. But you haven't flown for a commercial airline in five years."

"That's true. I was running my own business, but I fly every weekend. I've logged 500 hours in the last year. The truth is, I needed a change."

As she knew only too well, people who chose to live in a place like Spruce Bay weren't your run-of-the-mill types. They were adventurers, dreamers, people who were running away from any number of things. They were different.

Max didn't really seem all that different. But she caught the gleam of adventure in his eye. A thrill-seeker, she thought.

"I'll need to see you fly. Check your references. Then you'll have a second interview."

"Second interview?" He glanced around as though wondering where she was hiding the rest of the staff.

"My grandmother. She owns the business. She has the final say."

LYNETTE LOVED HIM. Not that Claire was surprised. When her grandmother heard the story of how Max had walked in while she was firing Frank Carmondy she laughed her earthy laugh. It was good to hear that sound after seeing her despair the previous day, but then Lynette was never one to stay in the dumps.

"It's not funny, Grandma. I am pretty sure Frank Carmondy was stealing from you."

"And he'll have to pay back whatever he stole. Maybe go to jail." Lynette was settled in an oak chair at her big, round kitchen table. It was where all important family business was conducted. "But I bet none of that would hurt his pride as much as getting fired by a little snip of a thing like you."

Very conscious that Max was there with them, Claire argued, "I am not a little snip of a thing. I'm a grown woman."

"When Frank first started working here you were, what, eighteen? He won't take kindly to the fact that it was you, a young woman, the granddaughter of the man who hired him, who gave him the boot." She cackled again, blue eyes twinkling. "Lord, I wish I could have seen his face." She stopped laughing. Looked Max over with her shrewd old eyes. "So, we lost one troublesome male and got ourselves another one, did we?"

"I'm here on approval, Ms. Lundstrom," he said. "If you don't agree to hire me, I'll get the boot too."

She chuckled again. "Well, he's smooth, I'll give him that," she said to Claire. "Good-looking, too. Looks like that Spanish fellow I like. What's his name?"

"Javier Bardem?"

"No. The other one."

"Antonio Banderas?"

"That's it. You Spanish, Max?"

"Argentinian. Well, my parents are. I was born in the States."

"Speak Spanish?"

"Yes. Also Portuguese and French."

"Could be handy with international passengers. If we ever had any."

She tapped her fingers against the arm of the chair. Her gold wedding ring was the only jewelry she wore. "How'd he do on the flight test?" she asked Claire.

"He's got good hands and feet. Knows his way around a plane." If he was uncomfortable with listening to them talk about him, Max gave no sign of it.

"Where you living?"

"I was going to look for a place in town."

She shook her head. "Tough to find accommodation. The rentals are awful and overpriced. You'd better have the caretaker's old quarters here on the property."

"Grandma," Claire said. "Don't you think we should talk about this?"

"I think that the sooner Frank Carmondy knows there's a man living on the property with us the better. He's got a temper on him, that one. Better he knows we're not unprotected."

Claire wondered what her grandmother was doing. The woman had been flying bush planes back when Betty Crocker was learning to cook. She'd faced down grizzlies, blizzards, drunken prospectors, lecherous passengers and she'd never once felt the need for a man's protection. Lynette could still shoot the *O* out of a Coke can at fifty feet. She'd taught Claire how to do the same. She did not need to be protected from a blustering bully of an ex-employee.

But Claire wasn't about to get into all that with Max sitting there, so she said, "It will take a couple of days to clean out the old place and get it habitable. There's a hotel downtown that will put you up for a few days."

He turned those liquid brown eyes her way. She suspected he heard subtext the way other people hear regular conversation. He nodded. "That's fine. I flew in. Is there a taxi?"

Before she could speak, Lynette said, "Claire will drive you into town. We pride ourselves on Northern hospitality."

Claire smiled through gritted teeth and decided she and her beloved grandmother were going to have a serious talk before too long. She strongly suspected there was some very unsubtle matchmaking going on. As she'd told her grandmother on many an occasion, simply because Lynette had married another bush pilot didn't mean Claire was going to follow suit.

She even made a point of dating men who kept both feet on the ground most of the time. She'd gone out with the town's only dentist, a tugboat captain and a mining engineer. All lovely, interesting men. Didn't matter. Lynette checked out every new bush pilot as though she were measuring him for his wedding tux.

"Come on," she said to Max. "I'll drive you into town."

"Did I pass the interview?" he asked as they headed to the old Yukon. The SUV was pitted with rust and caked with dust, but it was still as serviceable as when she'd learned to drive on it a dozen years ago.

"Are you kidding? She didn't just hire you. She practically adopted you. She never invites anyone to stay on the property."

She hiked herself up into the driver's seat. Max threw his duffel into the back and climbed in beside her.

"Is that a problem for you?"

She gazed at him. She was a pretty good judge of character and, if you didn't count Carmondy, she'd say her grandmother was even better. Her instincts told her that she could trust Max Varo. "No. It's not a problem."

They headed past the Cessna she knew was his.

"You brought your own plane?"

"Sure." He shrugged. "Like an old cowboy would bring his own horse."

She smiled. He must have saved for years to afford his own plane. She sensed he was as avid a flyer as she was. And that her grandmother was completely smitten.

As they rattled down the road she saw him looking out the dirt-specked window, at the runway, the ocean. "It's beautiful," he said.

"See if you still feel that way in January when the mercury dips below zero. That's when you find out if Spruce Bay is for you or not."

He glanced over at her. "And is it? For you?"

"Honestly? I can't imagine living anywhere else. Oh, sure, I love a trip to New York or L.A. to go shopping and eat in great restaurants, but I'm always glad to come back. Spruce Bay is in my blood."

Though it might not be in her family much longer if she didn't figure out how to save the business.

She pulled up to the Spruce Bay Inn. "This is the one I recommend. It's the priciest, but the beds are firm, the restaurant's good and they have Wi-Fi."

He turned to her and said, "Have dinner with me."

"What?"

The term *Latin lover* flitted through her mind when he turned the full force of those eyes and that charm on her. "Have dinner with me, tonight."

"I can't have dinner with you. I'm your boss."

"No. You're not. First, I don't start work until tomorrow. Second, Lynette told me she is my boss."

"I don't—"

"I understand if you prefer not to be seen with the hired help."

"It's not—I'm not a snob!"

When he smiled that slow, come-to-bed smile, she knew he had her. "I'm new in town. I have a lot of questions and I hate eating alone." He shrugged. "That's part of my heritage."

"It's just dinner," she told him.

"Of course."

She glanced at her watch. "It's four-thirty. Get a room and get settled. I'll come back at seven."

"Perfect. Thank you."

He got out of the Yukon, didn't seem to notice the way the door screeched when he opened it, pulled his bag out of the back, then leaned in and said, "Thanks for the ride. See you at seven."

She checked email on her phone for ten minutes, figured that should be enough time for Max to get settled in his room, and then walked into the inn. She walked straight past the front desk to the back offices, looking for the hotel manager.

Laurel Enright was her best friend and the person she most needed to talk to. Fortunately, she was in her office, talking on the phone. When she spied Claire she waved her in and made a face.

"No. I completely understand. Of course, a moose charging your car could make anyone miss their reservation. Absolutely. I quite understand. I don't blame your husband. I'd probably drink a bottle of scotch, too. Let's just be glad no one was hurt. Not even the moose. Of course I won't charge you for tonight. We'll look forward to welcoming you to the Spruce Bay Inn tomorrow. Uh-huh. You're welcome. You, too."

"Don't even ask," Laurel said when she put down the phone. She leaned forward. "I haven't seen you in ages. How are you?"

"Crazy busy, but good."

Laurel stood and walked around her desk. "Check out these babies. I bought them online."

Laurel was a vivacious redhead who'd been fighting to lose twenty pounds ever since Claire had known her. Claire thought she looked wonderful with her full breasts and hips, but she knew her friend didn't share her opinion. One thing they both agreed on, however, was that no matter how bad the climate, how deep the snowbanks or how sloppy the mud, shoes mattered. It had taken Claire a while to get used to carrying her good shoes in a shopping bag when she went out in the winter months, wearing her winter boots and parka and then changing into real shoes in the mudroom. But now she'd been doing it for so many years it seemed normal.

But it was summer now and Laurel had worn a kicking pair of cream half boots to work. "I love them."

"I know. Online shopping makes me feel a tiny bit less isolated. Too bad you can't mail-order men." She sighed and sat back down. "So, what brings you here?"

"I was dropping off our new pilot. He's going to stay here at the inn for a couple of days. Then Lynette wants him to move into the old caretaker's cottage."

"Hah. Is she trying to match you up with him?"

"Of course."

Laurel knew of her grandmother's attempts to get her attached to another bush pilot. "I think it's kind of sweet. She wants you to marry a pilot so you can take over Polar Air. Just like her and your grandfather."

"I know. I guess it is sweet, but it's also annoying. I'd like to pick my own men."

"What's he like?"

"His name is Max. His family's from Argentina, but he's American. He's…" How to describe the man? "He's very self-assured. Seemed like he didn't care whether he got the job or not, and yet he'd flown all the way up from Seattle for an interview. Good pilot."

"I don't want his résumé. I mean, what's he *like?*"

"Okay. He's hot. Really hot." She pushed her hair back. "He's also a bit pushy. He asked me for dinner."

"Already? You just met him."

"I know."

"Are you going?"

"He conned me. Made me feel like I'd be a snob if I didn't go out with him, like I thought I was too good for him since my family owns the company. So of course I said yes to prove him wrong."

"Well, the halibut is fresh tonight. Looks amazing." There was no question they'd be eating in the Inn dining room. It was the only decent place to eat in Spruce Bay.

"Thanks."

"I'll try and scope him out while he's here. I'm off tonight, so I can't hang around the bar and watch how your date is going."

"Thank goodness."

She chuckled. "Besides, I can't go near the restaurant. I'm on this juice diet. I see real food and I want to weep."

"How long does this juice diet last?"

"As long as I can stand it. I'm on day two. If I make day three I'm treating myself to a big steak dinner as a reward."

3

When Claire walked into the dining room of the Spruce Bay Inn, Max had a moment to enjoy the sight of her as she paused at the entrance to look for him. She was a truly lovely woman.

He hadn't been certain she'd show up, but here she was, and she'd dressed for dinner, he noted, in a flowered dress. Her legs were bare and her sandals celebrated the short summer season.

She'd left her hair long so it swung when she moved. He rose from his seat at the bar, walked to greet her.

Max reached for her hand.

"I wasn't sure you'd come," he said.

She gave him a sideways look. "I always keep my promises."

"Do you?" He thought of all the things he'd like her to promise him, decided he was getting ahead of himself. "Good."

He held out a chair for her and she seated herself across from him in the lounge.

"What are you drinking?" she asked.

"A caipirinha. It's Brazilian. Try it. Mostly rum and fruit juice." He held out his glass. She glanced up at him, then took the glass and sipped.

"Mmm," she said, then licked her lips. He felt a shaft of heat go right through him. If she'd done it deliberately to look sexy, the move would have left him cold. But her response was so natural, so unstudied that it caught at him. Made him wonder about how she might respond to other things.

What would she taste like when he kissed her? What kind of sounds would she make in bed? What would her skin feel like when he ran his fingers down her bare back? What did she look like when she came? The questions crowded his mind, as unbidden as they were inconvenient. He didn't want to fall for this woman. He was here for business reasons. And yet, from the moment he'd seen her in the office, both dainty and tough, giving a thieving employee his walking papers, he'd felt inexplicably drawn to her.

But Max was enough of a romantic to understand that passion couldn't be controlled or understood. You welcomed it when it came, like the bush pilots out here in Alaska welcomed the wild weather. You rode it, dove through it, embraced it.

"Would you like one?"

"Yes, please."

He motioned to their waitress and ordered her a drink.

"You're adventurous," he said when he'd given the order.

"And you're a charmer."

She said it matter-of-factly, not in an accusing way. So, he tried to consider whether he was, in fact, a charmer. "I don't consciously try to charm anyone."

"You certainly charmed my grandmother."

"I like your grandmother. She's an amazing woman."

She tilted her head to one side and her hair slid over her shoulders. "And I think you're trying to charm me."

"Do you suspect me of manipulation?" He shook his head. "It's not my intention. I like you. I think you're incredible. One day you'll be like your grandmother."

He could see she was pleased by the notion. "I hope so."

"And I also find you very beautiful."

"Definitely a charmer."

"A truth-teller," he corrected.

They moved to a window table for dinner. She ordered the halibut which their waitress told them was today's special. He ordered steak with Alaska king-crab legs and she laughed at him. "That's what the tourists order."

"It's my first day. Give me a break."

He kept things light. Asked her about her family, her life. Tried to imagine her orphaned in the critical teenage years. Coming here to live with her grandparents. He admired them for doing such a good job, and he admired her for overcoming tragedy and becoming the woman she was.

"I only wish I hadn't been an only child. It would have been nice to have a brother or sister to grow up with." She was solemn a moment, then gazed at him with those hazel eyes. "What about you? Family? Brothers and sisters?"

"My parents came to the States before I was born. My dad was an airline mechanic. My mother taught Spanish and looked after my sister and me.

"I had two best friends growing up, Dylan and Adam, who are still my best friends. My parents were strict, but they loved us. My sister's a teacher and she married a family friend. Moved back to Argentina."

"And you're a pilot."

"Yes," he said, because it was true. He was also a few other things, but there were some details he didn't feel ready to share with her. Like the fact that he had more money than he could ever spend. Or that his company was thinking of buying her airline.

As they were finishing their main course, he saw her glance over at the bar and stiffen. He followed her gaze. Frank Carmondy was there, drinking what looked like neat scotch and glaring at Claire.

Max felt a wave of irritation wash over him. Really? Did the man have to mess up his first date with this beautiful woman?

"Maybe we should leave," she said quietly.

"Maybe we shouldn't."

"I don't want to cause trouble for the people who run this hotel. They're friends of mine."

"Ignore him. If he chooses to make a scene it's his business. Maybe he'll have a drink and move on." He smiled at her. "Here, have a bite of crab. It's fantastic."

"If you're still here next April I'll cook you fresh king crab and you'll understand the difference." But she still opened her mouth and let him feed her a bite.

"Well?"

"Pretty good for frozen," she admitted.

Frank Carmondy banged his glass down on the bar and stormed over, as predictable as thunder after lightning. He came so close to their table he knocked into it and Max realized that scotch was far from his first.

"So, you fired me so you could give your boy toy my job, huh?"

Claire sent Max a sharp glance, essentially saying, "Let me handle this," so he kept his mouth shut and his temper in control.

"Frank," she said, "this isn't the time or place."

"You think you can fire me? Nobody fires me. You wouldn't have an airline without me."

The conversation in the dining room petered out as people turned to stare. Their waitress said something to a girl holding a water jug. She put down the water and hurried into the back, probably getting the manager. Even though Claire had told him to let her handle her ex-employee, Max found it difficult to sit still and stay out of the fray.

Carmondy slurred his words but they were loud and easy to understand. "I bet your grandmother's real happy you turned out to be such a slut. She used—"

Max was on his feet and had hold of one of Frank's beefy arms before he could finish the sentence.

He'd been prepared to let Claire handle the situation but he wasn't about to let a drunk insult her. Not while she was sitting having dinner with him at his invitation. He began to drag the man toward the exit.

"Where you think you're taking me?"

"Outside."

"Good," said a guy sitting with his wife at the next table. He glanced with dislike at the drunk former airline manager.

CLAIRE WASN'T THE type to swoon over a couple of guys brawling, she'd spent too long in Alaska for that, but she really didn't appreciate being at the center of controversy.

She was annoyed with Frank for being a drunk, stupid bully. Annoyed with Max for playing the hero yet again when no one had asked him to interfere.

She was annoyed with herself for agreeing to this

date. If she hadn't, the whole embarrassing situation would have been avoided.

She sipped her wine and gazed out the window. She should simply leave, but that would only add more drama to an already overwrought situation.

So, she sat. And waited.

It was a surprisingly short time later when Max returned. He didn't have a hair out of place or a wrinkle in his crisp white shirt.

He said, "I'm sorry for my absence. Would you like dessert?"

"No, thank you."

He picked up his napkin and neatly spread it over his lap when he reseated himself. "You're annoyed with me."

"I'm annoyed with you, with Frank, with me, with my grandfather for hiring such a creep."

"I know."

She fiddled with the stem of her wineglass. "What he said about me—"

She'd thought his eyes were the sexiest thing about him, but now that he was smiling at her so intimately, as though they shared secrets the rest of the world could never understand, she changed her mind. His smile was his sexiest attribute. "Please. I'm not stupid. You're a beautiful woman. He ever give you trouble?"

"He said a couple of inappropriate things. Nothing I couldn't ignore. Why?"

"Because if he did I'd have to rethink my earlier restraint."

A sound of frustration emerged from her throat. "You are from another century."

"Perhaps. Please join me in dessert."

"I never eat it. I'll have coffee."

"Fine."

When they were finished and he'd shaken off her offer to buy dinner as though it were an insult, she rose. "Thank you so much for dinner," she said.

"You're welcome." He walked out of the restaurant with her. She greeted people she knew as she passed, embarrassed that they'd all witnessed her encounter with Frank.

Max held the door that led to the gravel parking lot out front. And followed her through it.

She turned to him. "What are you doing?"

"I'm seeing you to your car."

"You're very old-fashioned."

"So I've been told."

Spruce Bay was far enough north that even at nine-thirty at night the sun hadn't set. There was plenty of light, making it easy to see the word *SLUT* scrawled with a finger in the dust on the Yukon's back window.

"Guess we need to wash the car more often," she said, digging in her bag for a tissue. Max was ahead of her, pulling a cotton handkerchief out of his pocket and wiping off the offensive word.

He didn't say anything, simply walked to the driver's side, waited until she'd unlocked the car, then opened the door and held it while she got in. She'd wondered if he'd attempt to kiss her. Hoped she'd be strong enough to resist. But he didn't. He slammed the door on her without a word.

So much for manners, she thought, putting her key in the ignition and firing up the beast.

The passenger door opened and to her shock, Max got in beside her.

She threw up both hands. "Now what are you doing?"

"Escorting you home."

"But you're staying at the hotel."

"Yes. I am."

"Max, this is ridiculous."

"I'm old-fashioned, remember?" And then she got it. He didn't want her going home alone in case Frank Carmondy wanted to cause more trouble than scrawling insults on her back window.

She looked at him. "You're going to drive me nuts, aren't you?"

His grin was both wolfish and understanding. "Probably."

THEY WERE MOSTLY quiet on the way home. John Mayer played on the radio. The old Yukon bumped and rattled on its way back to the barn. She felt Max's watchfulness but no drunken, crazed ex-employee jumped out at them.

She turned into the Polar Air property and all was serene.

She parked the car and turned to him, all sexy and mysterious beside her. "Well, Sir Galahad, it seems I'm home safe."

"Good." He began to lean toward her, slow and sure, but giving her plenty of time to pull back.

She did pull back, but not all the way. She put a hand to his chest, found it warm and muscular. "Even if I'm not your boss, we're still coworkers. This is against company policy."

"As I believe I mentioned, we're not coworkers until tomorrow."

He was so close she could see tiny black flecks in the deep brown of his irises, could smell the fresh laundry and hot male scent of him. Her lips began to open. She couldn't remember the last time she'd been this attracted to a man. "And what happens tomorrow?" she asked. Her voice came out breathless.

"We'll worry about that tomorrow," he said, and closed the last few inches between them, covering her mouth with his own.

His kiss was hot and sweet. Demanding and restrained. Such a mass of contradictions she found herself pulling him against her, demanding more.

He didn't need much encouragement. He plunged his hands into her hair, holding her so he could kiss her thoroughly. He licked into her mouth, teased her tongue. He tasted of the coffee they'd drunk, a hint of wine, and deeper of sexy, potent, demanding man.

A tiny cry came from her throat, part protest, part acquiescence. He was so hot. When she ran her hands over his chest and back she found that he was muscular and toned, as she'd guessed.

Seat belts were a hindrance. He snapped his free with a curse. Then reached and unsnapped hers.

He turned her toward him and let his own hands play. He didn't grab straight for her breasts, but traced the scoop of her neckline with one fingertip. Her nipples came to life. She felt them bloom against her dress, hard and insistent.

His single fingertip, seemingly oblivious, traced her shoulder, tracked to her upper back and moved up her spine into her hairline. She shivered. How had she never known how sensitive she was in that spot?

She copied his movement, lightly dragging her index finger into the V of his open shirt, so she touched warm, warm skin and springy hair. His subtle caress reminded her of how long it had been since she'd been touched like this.

No, she realized, she'd never been touched like this. Not with this slow abandon. This controlled madness.

"I don't think I've ever wanted anyone as much as I want you right now," he said, all huskiness and passion.

"Mmmm," she said.

"Come back to the hotel with me?"

She let her fingers play in his thick, gorgeous hair. "I can't," she almost wailed.

He kissed her one more time. Then broke away and pulled out his phone. "Do you know the number of a cab?"

"Take the car," she said, feeling breathless and out of control. "Bring it back in the morning."

He nodded. "Thanks."

She got out of the vehicle and found her legs were trembling. He came around the back and met her, reaching for her arms as though he couldn't stop himself from touching her. "I will dream of you tonight," he said, and kissed her; one last, lingering kiss.

As he drove away, she suspected he'd be in her dreams, too.

If she slept.

4

SPRUCE BAY WAS full of self-sufficient people who were proud of their toughness and ability to survive the harsh climate. Max discovered all of this as he strolled the town on foot, getting a feel for his home for the next while.

There were outdoor equipment stores, hunting and fishing shops as well as a Realtor, financial planners, a grocery store and a pharmacy.

He found the local rec center, where, due to the long winter, the main sports were curling, figure skating and hockey.

Needless to say, the ice rink was in perfect condition.

After some asking around, he tracked down the manager of the facility. "Hi," he said, "I'm Max Varo. New hire at Polar Air."

"I know who you are," the guy said. "Heard you took care of Frank Carmondy pretty good the other night."

Max had no idea whether this was a good or a bad thing in the other man's opinion. "He was bothering my date," he said.

The guy nodded. "Time somebody called him on his crap." He held out his hand. "Ted Lowenbrau. What can I do for you?"

"I need some ice time. I'm practicing for a big tournament. Badges on Ice."

"I've heard of it. We've sent a few teams from here over the years. They letting in pilots now? Thought you had to be a cop or a firefighter."

"The tournament's for emergency services, you're right. I'm an ambulance reserve guy. I play on a team with my buddies. We really need to keep up the practicing if we have a hope of winning." He wondered if he could fly Adam and Dylan up for a few sessions. Depending on his schedule, he might also be able to head south for the odd practice.

"What's your schedule like? Could I rent the rink for a few hours a week?"

"Be real early in the morning or late at night."

He nodded. "I'm used to that."

"Give me your details. We'll work something out."

"Thanks."

Max had already decided that he needed to keep up his workouts even without the Hunter Hurricanes. He figured he'd work out on his own, and if that didn't do the trick, he'd hire some kids from a local hockey team to practice with him. They'd get free ice time and he'd get to keep up his skills and fitness level. Everyone would be happy.

In the meantime, he started flying for Polar Air, getting to know the rest of the pilots, learning about each of the five aircrafts.

And, as promised, within three days, he had a place to live right on the Polar Air site. The caretaker's cottage was a small log cabin built of cedar. There was a bedroom, a living area, a kitchen, a bathroom with shower and a porch out front.

It looked as though it had been built in the '50s and

any updating had been minor. However, there was cable and Wi-Fi and the place came furnished. Max knew there were aspects of his own home he was going to miss, like his in-home gym, infrared sauna and top-of-the-line electronics. But he'd never been a man who needed luxury. He suspected he'd do just fine in his little cottage.

When Ted called him at the end of the week, he said, "I've got Tuesdays and Thursdays at 10:00 p.m. open. You get the ice for an hour."

"That's fantastic. Thanks."

"There's one other hockey player who will be on the rink at that time. I figure you can do drills together or skate around each other or something."

"Yeah. Sure. Sounds good." He hoped the other guy was as good as he was. Maybe they could work together, spur each other on.

Maybe even have a beer together once in a while.

MAX FELL INTO A routine over the next few weeks. There were twelve pilots altogether. The planes, a fleet of Beavers and Cessnas, serviced fishing lodges and dropped mail, supplies and parts to mining and logging operations. They also transported hunters and hikers and geologists and photographers and anybody who wanted to fly someplace in Alaska.

Lynette was often on duty at the office. But Claire made sure she was around regularly as well. Max saw how protective she was of her grandmother while trying not to let it show to anyone, least of all to Lynette.

Max was the perfect employee, efficient, respectful, always willing. Claire was wary around him, a little jumpy, he suspected because of the kisses they'd shared and the sizzle that burned the air between them whenever they were together. He wasn't a man who would ever regret kissing a beautiful woman, but he admitted to himself that having tasted her it was impossible not to want more.

However, he knew the next move would be up to her, so he got on with his job and tried to keep his fantasies about Claire to a respectable minimum.

He liked the work. Enjoyed flying terrain he wasn't familiar with. Liked the other pilots, though he didn't want to get too close to them. He knew something they didn't: that he'd likely own the company they worked for at some point in the near future. He didn't want to earn their contempt by pretending to be one of them when it was only temporary.

He kept in touch with his assistant daily, but Varo Enterprises was running as smoothly as he'd expected it would.

And he was having fun. He loved turnarounds. Didn't matter to him that this was a much smaller company than most he'd worked on recently. He liked being on the ground—and in the air—seeing the potential.

What he didn't like was seeing the crease between Claire's brows. He suspected she hadn't known about the mortgage being called until recently. He knew that with the purchase price he had in mind for Polar Air she and her grandmother would be able to pay off the mortgages and still have enough left over for a decent life. But he didn't want to tell her who he was. Not yet. If he decided not to buy Polar Air he didn't want her to be disappointed.

So he kept his mouth shut and his eyes open.

He spent some of his downtime getting to know Spruce Bay. It wasn't a big town and in a lot of ways it had let progress pull out into the fast lane and speed on by, leaving it puttering along contentedly at its own slow pace.

One thing soon became clear. He needed a vehicle if he was going to spend any time at all here. He got a ride into town with Will Runningbear, a younger pilot. "I need to buy a truck, Will. Where do you suggest?"

"You got two choices. Spruce Bay Motors if you want a new vehicle or if you want to get ripped off on a used one. Or you can go to Tough Beans and look at the notice board. Most everything gets posted there."

"What about Craigslist?"

Will shrugged large shoulders. "You can try."

So, Max got Will to drop him off at Tough Beans. As promised, there was a big cork notice board offering apartment rentals, jobs, massage therapists, financial planners and guys to clean out your gutters or remove snow. And there was a section where people were advertising goods for sale from property to bowling shoes. There were three trucks on offer. One was fifteen years old and so full of rust he figured it would need to be towed, not driven. The second truck was too new and shiny. Truck number three was a five-year-old F-150. Mileage looked reasonable and the condition was listed as good. He called the number on his cell phone.

Within hours he was the proud owner of a Ford truck. He drove it back to the property and parked behind the small house they'd given him.

THE NEXT MORNING he walked into the office at six-thirty and headed straight for the coffee machine. Claire was already there, sitting behind one of the desks, tapping at a computer. "Morning, Claire."

"Morning, Max."

She rose, and walked over to stand beside him. She seemed ill at ease.

"Everything all right?"

"I don't know. Look, I'm not one to pry into other people's business but I'm wondering how you managed to pay cash for a truck yesterday. That's a lot of money on a bush pilot's salary."

He cursed himself for a fool. Of course this was a town where gossiping was as common as breathing. He could imagine the speculation going on behind her pretty eyes. Knew he'd be doing the same if their positions were reversed.

He stirred cream into his coffee, added two sugars. Then he leaned back against the counter, took a sip of the brew. "I had some money sitting in an account." It was true enough. "I came by that money honestly. Don't worry, I'm not another Frank Carmondy."

She gazed at him searchingly. "Okay."

He felt twitchy inside. He didn't like hiding things from Claire. He didn't want to mislead a woman he liked, especially one who was suffering because of a crooked employee. He couldn't raise false hopes though, not until he was sure Polar Air was a sensible acquisition for his company. And the fact that he had a crush on the owner's granddaughter was not a sound reason to rush into this deal. Not for his management team or for himself.

She turned to go back to her computer but he felt her unease. She deserved to know more. "I'm not a poor man." He shrugged his shoulders. "In fact, I'm pretty good with money. Okay? My family raised me to be careful. They never had any debt apart from their mortgage, which they paid off as soon as they could by hard work and saving. Those habits are hard to break. In fact, no matter how much money I had, I wouldn't want to."

His reward for telling her a little of the truth was seeing her relief. "Your parents sound like my grandparents. They only ever borrowed money for land and equipment. They worked so hard to build this airline." He saw her hand clench into a fist and knew she was thinking of the man who had stolen so much of that hard-earned wealth. The man who had put the entire company's future into jeopardy, if Leslie's sources were to be believed.

Of course, Claire had no idea how much he already knew.

"Is it bad?" he asked gently, wanting her to trust him.

For a second he thought she might blurt it all out. There was a moment of vulnerability on her face and she opened her lips. Then, she must have reconsidered. As he watched emotions flit across her face, he was fairly certain he could tell what she was thinking. He was only a new hire, after all. They'd enjoyed dinner together and some hot, steamy kissing in the old Yukon, but could she really trust him?

She gave a firm shake of her head. "Not too bad. I promise your paycheck won't bounce."

A wise man would nod, make a wisecrack and back away. But he couldn't let it go at that. He thought he understood how much the financial difficulty was hurting her. Since her grandparents and his folks obviously shared a loathing of debt he could only imagine how he'd feel if somebody swindled his mom and dad and he felt helpless to fix it.

He put his two hands on her shoulders and squeezed gently. "You can trust me, Claire. That I promise."

When she looked at him like that he wanted to pull

her to him and kiss her, to tell her he was her knight in shining armor, here to save her airline, make sure there was enough money for Lynette to enjoy her retirement in comfort and for Polar Air to continue to operate with its books balanced and its reputation restored.

The moment hovered, he moved a tiny bit closer, she tilted her head in his direction. He could already taste her lips.

The bell on the door jangled, pulling them both sharply back to reality. What was he thinking? He didn't make business decisions based on a pair of big hazel eyes and the sweetest lips he'd ever kissed. He needed to get a grip.

They both greeted Will, also headed for the coffee machine. Claire gave Max his schedule for the day. He was doing a food-and-supply drop-off for a group of hikers. He understood that she was giving him the least challenging runs until she felt confident that he could handle more.

It was a funny thing to realize he wanted to prove to her that he could handle more.

How long had it been since he'd been forced to prove himself?

Max wondered if he'd grown soft, too accustomed to having people agree with him and suck up to him because of his wealth. He suspected the experience of showing Claire and the rest of the Polar Air team that he was good enough to fly their toughest routes would be good for him.

Whatever ended up happening with Polar Air he knew one thing.

He was no longer bored.

5

When Tuesday evening arrived, Max pulled together his hockey bag, threw it in the back of his new truck and headed for the town rink. He was early, so he had a few minutes to watch the tail end of a figure skating class. The eight girls and two boys were at all ages and levels but he watched a few moves that impressed the hell out of him. He supposed in a town where winter dominated, ice sports were the best way to keep kids out of trouble.

After the skaters left the ice the Zamboni rolled onto the surface and he headed to the men's change room to get suited up.

When he emerged onto the empty rink, he wondered how the Hunter Hurricanes were doing without him. He knew he was going to have to get back for a few games or he'd lose his spot on the team. Much as Dylan, Adam and he were the best front line the Hurricanes had ever had, he knew they'd replace him if he didn't get down there regularly.

He decided right then what he needed to do, and before he could forget or change his mind, he pulled out his cell phone and sent a text to Dylan and Adam. Need you guys to come practice with me in Spruce Bay. See if you can work it into your schedules. You know you'll never win BOI without me.

He sent the text and wondered if they'd come. Knew he had to entice them with more than a rink in Alaska. Sent a second text. Really hot women here. He thought of Claire and smiled.

He stepped onto the ice, warmed up a little and then practiced power skating. He turned to his left, turned to his right. He was stronger on his right side, could shoot much tighter.

He could buttonhook around on the right, but going to the left took thought and effort so he practiced both. He practiced crossovers. He'd start on the goal line, skate to the blue line, back to goal then past blue to center, then back to the goal line in figure eights that grew increasingly fast. He slowed down when he became aware of another person entering the rink.

He slowed and glanced up, wondering who the other guy was and if they'd be able to practice together. Then he realized it was a woman. And she was wearing a pink helmet. Ted Lowenbrau had made him think he'd be practicing with another guy.

She stilled when she saw him. He noticed her compact, curvy body and as she began coming toward him he realized it was a very familiar shape.

"Claire?" he said when she skated closer. "What are you doing here?"

"I was going to ask you the same question. I always practice at this time."

"Ted Lowenbrau, the guy who runs the rink, told me I could practice Tuesdays and Thursdays. He said there'd be somebody else to do drills with. He didn't mention it was you."

She made a frustrated sound. "You'd think you were the only man in Spruce Bay and I was a desperate spinster," she snapped. "In fact, there are far more men here than women. I happen to be particular, that's all."

Since she'd seen fit to have dinner with him and do some seriously nice kissing and fondling, he decided that this was a compliment.

SHE NEVER SHOULD have had dinner with him, Claire thought. She'd known it the moment Max asked her out, but the combination of her bad afternoon with Frank, and the chance to get to know her new impulse hire, had won out against common sense. Also, as she couldn't help noticing, he was hot.

So, she'd dressed up and gone to dinner.

And this was the result. Guys like Ted, who'd be too busy come ice-fishing season to give her a thought, had decided to do a little matchmaking.

For all she knew, her darling grandmother had put Ted up to it.

There were times that Claire longed to live in a nice big anonymous town like New York where nine million people didn't know your name and didn't care about your business. No, she thought, Mumbai, that's where she'd go. The weather was better and most of the nineteen million inhabitants didn't speak English, making it more difficult for her neighbors to interfere in her personal life.

She adjusted her helmet.

Apparently the people of her town were right since Max hadn't made a single attempt to get close and personal with her after that one steamy kiss—when was it, two weeks ago? She said, "Probably a prank."

Max rested his chin on the top of his stick. Regarded her. "You any good?"

She kept her features schooled. She'd gone to college on a hockey scholarship. Been scouted for the women's Olympic team. She could kick his ass on the ice from here to Sunday. But he didn't have to know that.

She toggled her hand back and forth. "Not bad for a girl. You?"

"I've never played hockey with a woman. I don't want to hurt you."

She knew it was foolish of her to care that he hadn't asked her out again or tried to increase the intimacy after that one steamy kiss. A kiss that had been so unforgettable she had trouble thinking about anything else when he was around. While he seemed to have completely forgotten the experience.

So, she was foolish. Max wanted to play it cool. That was fine by her. But here they were on a rink, which, second to sitting in a cockpit in midair, was the place she felt most at ease. Was she good enough? Hah! She decided she was going to enjoy herself.

In Moscow at an international college championship she'd shot a puck that had been clocked at 80 mph. She said, "Let's take it slow. I'll try to keep up."

Normally, she shot left, but she transferred her stick to the other hand, knowing that he was the one most likely to get hurt if she didn't watch herself.

"Sure. What do you want to practice?"

"Let's try some passing."

"Okay."

They started slowly with some soft passes, then they tried passing on the move and soon they were into hard passes, back passes, open-ice passes.

He wasn't bad, she admitted to herself as she watched him move. He had the natural grace of a born athlete, was quick on his feet, with good skills and an easy way with the stick.

In spite of herself, she was impressed.

SHE WAS GOOD for a girl, Max thought, impressed in spite of himself. She skated smoothly, as though she'd been born on skates. Which, considering she'd grown up in Spruce Bay, was probably true. She was a little tentative shooting the puck and she sometimes stopped to scan the ice as though trying to figure out where he was and where the net was, but those were things that improved with practice.

And clearly, she liked to practice.

"What are you practicing for?" he asked, when they took a quick water break.

"I like the exercise," she said as she skated by. "And for me shooting pucks is good stress relief. You?"

"I'm part of an emergency-services league team. I need to stay in shape. We want to win the championship game this year."

"Since when is a pilot part of emergency services?"

"I'm also a reserve ambulance attendant. Two of my oldest friends play on the same league so they let me stay."

"Sounds like fun." She glanced at him. "So, you'll need time off?"

"Yeah. But it's months away. There's lots of time."

At the end of an hour they were both breathing heavily. She didn't know when it had happened but slowly she'd let go of her control and he'd matched her. Now they were both putting a little effort into the practice and she was having fun.

When the clock showed it was eleven o'clock she realized the time had flown by. Usually by the end of practice she was fighting boredom.

Not tonight.

"That was fun," she said.

"It was. And you are a hell of a lot better than 'not bad.' You could beat half the guys on my team."

"Thanks."

He skated up until he was standing in front of her, blocking her exit. "Want to go for a beer?"

"Is that what you do with your buddies after practice?" She removed her pink helmet, gave her head a shake so her ponytail settled down her back.

"Sometimes."

She glared up at him. "I am not your buddy."

Little puffs of white came out of her mouth as she said the words. She was still breathing fairly hard. This was the best workout she'd had in months.

"I know. But I can't figure out what the hell you are. My coworker? My boss? My hockey practice partner?" He shook his head. "Not what I want you to be." His eyes seemed to caress her face and she felt warmth all around her in spite of the cold rink.

Her heart jumped stupidly. "No?"

"No."

There was a slight buzzing sound coming from the industrial lights above them, otherwise the world was cold and silent. She said, "What do you want me to be?"

He moved closer, so smooth on the ice she'd barely noticed. "I want to be your lover."

Even as her heart skipped a beat, she said, "You've got a funny way of showing it. You act like the other night never happened."

She felt his gaze increase in intensity. "Oh, it happened. And it's going to happen again."

He wrapped one arm around her, pulled her closer and kissed her.

His lips were cold and he tasted of sweat, but she didn't care. In seconds they were warm and as seductive as she remembered. A tiny sound came out of her throat and she slid forward, so close their skates touched. It had been so long since she'd felt this potent rush of want, need and passion that wouldn't be denied. Her last relationship, with the dentist, had ended six months ago when he'd got a better offer and relocated to Minneapolis. She had missed him a little. They'd managed a few weekends together and then he'd asked her to move to be with him, and she knew then that she didn't care enough about him to give up her life here in Spruce Bay. Frankly, she doubted she'd ever love a man enough to leave her home, her job and her family. Which made Max a tantalizingly attractive prospect.

He worked in her business, lived right on the property. Her grandmother would be thrilled.

Which was exactly why she had to be so careful.

That's what her rational mind was thinking.

Her body was reminding her that she was a young, healthy woman and she hadn't had sex in almost six months.

She pulled away from the sexiest mouth she had ever kissed. "I have to shower," she said, knowing it ought to be a cold one.

Max flashed his killer grin. "Me, too. But I don't want to let you go."

"I'm not going far."

He tilted his head to the side, arms still loosely wrapped around her. "Come back to my place?"

She shook her head. "Everybody in town would know by breakfast time tomorrow."

"Then take me back to your place."

She bit her lip, wishing she could, knowing she shouldn't. "I can't. The crew will figure it out right away."

"No, they won't. They'll come to work in the morning and I'll already be hard at it. They'll think I'm a keener, a brown-noser. Not that I spent the night with you."

She'd wanted to know that he still thought about her, still found her attractive. But now that he was suggesting a night in her bed she felt suddenly unsure.

He gazed at her evenly. "I'm not that guy, you know. The one who boasts about his conquests."

Instinctively, she knew he was telling the truth. She shook her head. "It's not that. I just—" She let out a breath that puffed like smoke in the cold rink. "It's a small town. We work together. What if—"

He kissed her before she could finish the sentence. When he pulled away, he said, "What if you stop worrying so much about the future and think about enjoying the present."

Oh, how she wanted to. She knew somehow that he'd be amazing in bed. It was the way he looked at her, as though he genuinely appreciated and enjoyed women. The way he moved, athletic and graceful. The way he kissed.

She was a young woman in her prime and she loved sex. Right now she was so hot she was grateful that the rink was cool enough to stop her from exploding on the spot.

Finally, she said, "I'm not ready." And found, in spite of the incredibly strong attraction between them, that it was true. She wasn't ready.

Instead of arguing, as she'd half expected him to, he said, "I understand. But, just so you know, I am so ready I can hardly stand it."

She smiled, because she was flattered and horny and enjoying the feeling of being attracted to a man for the first time in a while.

He took off his right-hand glove, reached out and touched her face. "When you're ready, all you have to do is lift a finger, an eyebrow, a strand of hair, and I'll be there."

She chuckled, thinking of all the times it got windy in Spruce Bay. "A strand of hair, huh?"

"Figuratively speaking," he replied with dignity.

"Okay."

"Go shower. I'll meet you out front. At least let me walk you to your car."

He was so old-fashioned in some ways that it made her smile. "Deal."

As they walked out together, he said, "Any more messages from your former manager?" He glanced pointedly at the spot where the word *SLUT* had been scrawled on the rear window of the Yukon Max's first night in town.

"No. But he's asked me to meet with him."

Max's brows rose. "Not his lawyer?"

"No. He wants a meeting with only the two of us."

"Where and when?" He said the words sharply and she realized that Max was being protective again.

"I'm not stupid, Max. He's coming to the office."

"When?"

"Look, I appreciate that you're trying to protect me, but I've been managing fine on my own. I'm grown up, independent and can handle one ex-employee without having to cast myself on your big chest for help."

Instead of taking offense, he grinned, puffed out his chest in an exaggerated fashion and said, "You noticed."

She laughed, but still didn't give him the information he wanted.

"Okay," he said. "But promise me if he gets out of

line or you don't like the way he's talking to you that you'll call me."

"No. I won't. If he in any way makes me uncomfortable I'll call the sheriff. We've known Frank for years." She felt regret pull at her. Frank had been part of Polar Air almost as long as she had. She couldn't bear the thought that he'd stolen from them or that she might have to press charges against the man who'd been as much a family friend as an employee.

"Hey," he said, as though reading her thoughts, "I'm sure it won't come to anything."

"Yeah."

"You sure you won't change your mind?" he asked as she opened the Yukon's door.

She wavered, looking into those dark, sexy eyes and reliving for a moment the feel of his body against hers, his mouth teasing and promising. But resolutely she shook her head.

"Rain check," she said.

6

MAX WATCHED THE old Yukon bounce and rumble its way out of the parking lot and onto the main street.

Rain check. What kind of an expression was that anyway? All it conjured up in his mind was an image of him and Claire in a cabin somewhere. Or a loft with skylights. A tropical hut in the jungle. Someplace where the rain would pound down around them. He imagined her, naked and passionate, while water pattered on the roof and her sighs mingled with the sounds of a storm raging.

He had to shake his head to clear it. What the hell was wrong with him?

Max had been singularly lucky in his life and he knew it. He'd always liked women. Maybe because he adored his mother and even though he hadn't always adored his bossy older sister, he still loved her. Knew she had his back as he had hers.

But the combination of his financial success at such a young age and his genuine appreciation of women had meant that he hadn't encountered many challenges in his dealings with the opposite sex.

He met lots of women. Polished beauties who were

only too happy to trade their undeniable physical assets for the more worldly assets he could provide, high-powered businesswomen who were colleagues and sometimes more. But in every case, who he was—and what he could offer—were a part of the attraction.

It wasn't that he'd ever fantasized about a prince-and-the-pauper scenario, where he could pretend to be poor and find a girl who would love him for who he was rather than his wealth and position. In fact, he thought the idea was ludicrous.

Still, it was a refreshing change to find himself in a place where no one knew or cared who he was, to feel that his net worth didn't enter the room ahead of him.

As he drove back to the hotel in his new-to-him truck, he realized that he was enjoying being Max the bush pilot. Not Max the boss, not Max the guy who could write a check that would make a charity hostess weep, not Max the genius billionaire.

Here, he was just Max.

Oddly, he liked being seen for who he was alone. He found it relaxing to have so few expectations thrust upon him. To be able to fly most of the day.

And he liked very much not having to wonder whether a woman's interest in him was influenced by his bank account balance, his connections, his place in the business community. He wanted to know that a woman might like him for himself.

Maybe he'd become like one of those entitled rich guys he couldn't stand. Because he realized, when Claire had turned him down, that he hadn't had to try this hard to get a woman for a very long time.

Did she intrigue him so much because she was a challenge and he was spoiled? He thought back to the way she'd felt in his arms on the ice. They'd both worn practice gear and skates. They were both perspiring and not exactly at their most attractive, but still he'd pulled her to him, needing the connection.

Lust lunged through him at the memory, pure and hot.

No, he thought. Claire wasn't appealing because she didn't know who he was, or because she wasn't in a hurry to sleep with him. Claire's appeal lay with Claire herself.

He liked her toughness and the vulnerability she worked so hard to hide. He liked her work ethic. He'd seen the hours she put in and how many of the tougher flights she took.

He liked the way she took care of her grandmother without Lynette quite realizing it. Family was extremely important to Max and he liked that Claire felt the same way.

He liked the frank way she looked at him, her curvy body and the way she carried so much responsibility on her slim shoulders.

He didn't like the fact that Frank Carmondy was allowed back on the property, he thought to himself as he bounced over a pothole he hadn't seen coming. If it had been up to him, the guy would be facing criminal charges right now. But he had to accept that it wasn't his decision.

All he could do was hang around as much as he could and keep an eye on Claire, especially if that thieving lowlife came around to see her.

No, he thought, he could do more than that. One of the companies Varo Enterprises owned was a security firm.

When he got back to his cottage, he sent a message

to his top security guy asking that he quietly check out Frank Carmondy and get back to him. ASAP.

He was coming up on three weeks in Spruce Bay. He liked living on the Polar Air property where he could at least try to protect two women he'd grown to like and admire. He even liked his little cottage and cooking the few meals he didn't grab out.

He took a few minutes so that Claire could arrive home ahead of him and leave no material for idle gossip.

Adam and Dylan had replied to his text. Seemed they wanted to Skype him.

As soon as he was home and showered, he opened the connection. Found his two buddies.

They were at Dylan's apartment, obviously sharing a beer after practice. "You should be here," Dylan said, by way of greeting. He lifted a cold one and Adam did the same.

"Wait a minute," he said, and reached for the small fridge in his kitchen. Came out with a local IPA. Took off the cap, saluted them and drank deep of the cold brew.

"What's all this about hot girls?" Dylan asked immediately. Max wasn't sure whether he wanted to know so he could try and bag one of the hot girls in question or whether he was hoping Max would finally give up the joys of being single so he could win their bet. Hard to say with Dylan. He could be after either one. Or both at the same time.

"Well, I found a hot one."

"Yeah? She give you the time of day?"

"As a matter of fact I was out with her tonight."

"What were you doing?"

"We played hockey."

Adam stopped with his bottle halfway to his mouth.

Dylan choked. "Dude, you've been in Alaska too long."

There was a pause. Adam said, "He's playing with you, Dyl."

Max shook his head. "No. I'm not. She really does play hockey."

"What else does she do?" Adam asked. Smart guy, Adam. No wonder he was a detective.

"She's also my boss. Sort of. She basically runs Polar Air. She's a pilot."

"A hockey-playing bush pilot," Dylan said slowly. "She chew tobacco, too? Hunt moose? Wrestle grizzlies?"

He felt a smile pulling at his lips. "You guys need to come up and meet her."

"We need to do an intervention."

"How are you liking it up there?" Adam asked after they both ignored Dylan.

"It's great. Beautiful, unspoiled wilderness. I've seen the Northern Lights. People are friendly, mostly."

"Do you miss your regular life?"

"No. I was thinking about it earlier. You know in that story about the prince and the pauper, how the rich guy and a poor one trade places? Well, I've done that in a way. I'm seen as a much simpler man here, and I like it."

Dylan spoke again. "So, you're dating a hockey player and you think you're living in a fairy tale. I'm definitely thinking an intervention is in order."

Once more Adam and Max ignored him. "Won't she find out who you are?"

"Sure, eventually. I mean, I'll tell her, obviously. But I'm not a very high-profile guy. I'm not a big self-promoter or media hound so I can't imagine how she'd find out I'm more than just a bush pilot. I'll tell her I'm the guy thinking of buying her airline. But right now I don't want to get her hopes up. I don't want her to be disappointed if Polar Air ends up not making economic sense for my company. Besides, it's nice getting to know a woman without all that baggage in the way."

"Yeah, those bags of million-dollar bills sure do weigh a guy down."

"Do you need a loan or something?" Max snapped. Dylan was being particularly Dylan tonight.

"Don't mind him. He's pissed because we missed you at practice tonight. It's not the same."

"Yeah. I know. I'm going to see if I can work my day off around hockey practice so I can at least get down there once a week. Did you think about my offer? I could fly you guys up here for a few practices."

"Max, we need you here. There are a lot of guys who want to take your spot."

Of course there were. "I'm hoping to have this wrapped up in a few weeks."

"Well, if you can get down here that would be great. We can try and come up to you, too."

"Yeah. To do an intervention!"

7

CLAIRE WAS ON her own in the office when the front door opened and Frank Carmondy walked in.

Even though he'd told her he was coming, her first impulse was to grab the shotgun she kept locked in her office. Her second was to grab the phone and call the sheriff. But one look at his face told her he wasn't here to cause trouble. Frank looked gray and ashamed and something she'd never seen before. He looked old.

"What can I do for you, Frank?"

"I—I owe you an apology."

"For what? Stealing money from the company or for scrawling insults on my car?" She kept her voice even but she still felt angry at the way he'd betrayed her family and the childish, vulgar way he'd lashed out at her.

He licked his lips as though he were very thirsty. "For all of it." His gaze dropped before hers and an unwelcome sense of pity washed over her.

"I've been waiting to hear from your lawyer," she said.

"You won't. That was all crap. I came here to tell you that. I—I did some things I'm ashamed of."

"You stole money, Frank. Quite a lot of it." And the

knowledge that Polar Air was in serious trouble because of his theft gnawed at her. "We've got suppliers we've dealt with for decades who extended credit because of my grandparents' reputations. You traded on that. That's how we never found out there was a problem until too late. And you kept increasing the bank line of credit until they called the loan."

"I know. And I'm going to pay every cent back. I promise. See, the thing is, I have a problem. I've been gambling. It got way out of control."

"Gambling?" In a town with no secrets how had she never discovered he was a gambler? "I never heard that."

"I wouldn't do it here where every fool knows your business. I—I gamble online mostly. Go to Vegas and Reno on my time off."

She thought of the trips he'd been taking down south twice a year, sometimes more often. "I thought you were visiting your son?"

He made a sound of disgust. "My son hasn't spoken to me in years. His mother turned him against me. I—" He licked his lips again. "Gambling makes me feel good, I guess. I drink a little, too, when I'm online. Helps me focus. But sometimes I forget how much I've bet. That's how I got into trouble. But I've learned my lesson now. I've stopped the gambling. I mean to pay you back. Every cent."

"Frank, I took a close look at the books. You've helped yourself to more than half a million dollars that I've identified so far. I'm guessing there's more."

His lip wobbled. "Please," he said. "Please don't go to the cops. I'm going to change. I am. I'm getting help. And I'll set up a series of payments. You'll get your money back. All of it. With interest."

"I don't know, Frank. I'll need to talk to Lynette about this."

He hung his head. "That makes me feel so much worse. With her heart condition, she shouldn't be bothered by this burden."

He was right, of course, but he might have considered Lynette's health before he started embezzling, she thought.

The outer door bell rang, indicating somebody had come into the office. As she was the only one there, she excused herself and went out front.

It was Arnie, one of the pilots, with his time sheet.

"Great, thanks."

Arnie was in his mid-thirties and his wife was expecting their second child. He took every extra shift he could get in order to help support his growing family. He said, "What's up for tomorrow?"

She mentally scanned the jobs coming up.

"Let's see. We need to get a piece of equipment to Westhaven mine. I'll do that one. You can take the Joyner party up to the fishing lodge."

"Is that the equipment in that crate?" He pointed to the large box in the corner that had been dropped off earlier for transport to the mine.

"Yep. That's it."

"It's too heavy for you to load and unload."

"I know. It's a two-person job. I'm taking Max with me. He can help with the heavy lifting, and it will give me a chance to show him the route. Introduce him to the people at the mine."

He nodded. "Sounds good. I gotta head off to prenatal class with the wife. See you tomorrow."

She returned to her office and Frank continued as though she'd never left.

"I quit drinking, too. You can ask anybody. I joined AA."

"That's good, Frank."

Finally, he said, "Well, like I said. I'm sorry. Why don't you take a few days to think about it? Maybe we could get together again and work out a repayment schedule."

"But how will you repay the money? You don't have a job." She hoped he wasn't expecting a good reference because she couldn't give him one.

"I'll sell my house. I've mortgaged it to gamble, but if I sell it there'll be enough to pay you back most of what I owe."

Then, from the bag he was carrying, he pulled out a framed photograph. "You probably want this back," he said and placed it in front of her on the desk. The photograph showed a much younger Frank with Claire and both her grandparents. Her grandfather had presented her with a company pin after she'd passed her first flight test. She remembered that day. It had been a hot August afternoon. They'd ended it with a barbecue. She'd been so proud and they all looked so happy.

Of course, she knew that Frank was deliberately manipulating her—she wasn't stupid. Still, it was impossible to gaze at that picture and not remember better times.

Gambling was a serious addiction, she knew. Like alcohol or drugs, it took over a person, caused them to do things that were out of character. She glanced at the man sitting across from her. Had he really reformed?

"I need to think about this, Frank. What you did is serious. We could lose the business. Lynette is devastated."

He stood heavily. "Understood."

He held out his hand and, after hesitating a moment, she took it. "When can we talk again?" he asked.

"I'm seeing our lawyer on Wednesday. I'll get some advice. If she agrees to a payback schedule, then I'll get you to work it out with her." That made the most sense to Claire. She didn't want to be trying to negotiate how and when he was going to pay back the money he stole. Much better to let their lawyer do it. Even though she hadn't talked about it with Lynette yet, she was pretty sure her grandmother would agree. She'd want to give Frank the benefit of the doubt.

"I'll get back to you by the end of the week."

"I appreciate your consideration, Claire. I really do."

She nodded, sad, and wishing he'd made some smarter choices along the way. But he hadn't, and they were in a fix. She wondered how much he could really pull out of his house if he'd been using it as an ATM machine all these years. And would it be enough to keep the bank off their backs, at least until she could improve business?

BECAUSE SHE FELT such a rush of pleasure when she saw Max striding toward her the next morning, she acted more crisp and businesslike than she would with any other pilot. She couldn't help herself.

He didn't seem fazed by her abrupt manner. If anything, he was amused.

He always looked so put-together and neat it was a wonder to her. He could fly for a thousand miles, spend hours cramped in the pilot's seat of a Beaver and emerge as though he'd somehow stopped en route to have all his clothing dry-cleaned and pressed. Amazing.

She felt creased and disheveled by comparison.

He helped her load and secure the crate headed for the mine.

She went through her before-takeoff checklist. She walked around the plane checking for any dents or problems. Checked her tires. She moved the ailerons up and down, made sure they were working properly. She checked the elevator, the critical piece of equipment at the back of the plane that would keep the aircraft level, for full play up and down. She checked that her emergency locator transmitter, or ELT, was on. Then she ticked off each item, saying it aloud as her grandfather had taught her to do. Since Max was there, she figured it didn't hurt for him to double-check that she got everything. "Auxiliary fuel pump, off. Flight controls, free and clear. Instruments and radios, checked and set. Altimeter, set. Directional gyro, set." She checked the fuel gauges and the trim set, checked the props were clear.

She jumped into the pilot seat and Max settled into the copilot seat beside her. They both donned headsets and belted in.

Before she started the engine, she opened her window and yelled, "Clear prop." She started the engine and while it was warming up she did her run up, bringing up the throttle. Checked her magnetos, right and left, engine idle. Set her flaps to ten degrees. She said, "I'll take her up and why don't you fly us home?"

"Happy to oblige, boss."

She called in to the control center to file her flight plan and then they were ready.

She radioed out: "This is Whiskey Alpha Bravo taking off on runway one-niner from Spruce Bay."

Once they were in the air and headed north, they flew in companionable silence punctuated by her pointing out features of the landscape and checking in with Lynette now and then via radio.

"I got a call from a tugboat company, they want us to fly out some log loaders, over."

"When do they need to fly? Over."

"First thing tomorrow. Can you do it?"

"Roger that."

Every unexpected flight meant a little more financial breathing room and she welcomed the extra work.

Today's flight would take them just over two hours, she calculated, with the fair winds at their back. A little longer on the return journey. The terrain they were flying over was intimately familiar to her after so many years, but of course it would all be new to Max so she tried to fill him in as they flew.

He was an interested and engaged companion. He asked her several questions about the history of the company, then suddenly asked, "Have you thought about partnering with some of the fishing lodges to offer packages?"

She imagined this was how it had been for her grandparents when they started Polar Air. The back-and-forth of two people in business together, with the same commitment to success they'd show in raising a family. For a second she understood why her grandmother was so keen for Claire to marry another pilot.

"Yes, of course we've considered it." She wondered how many opportunities they'd lost in the years that Frank had been running things. Refused to take refuge in blaming the former manager. "The truth is, we need to do more of that if we're going to—" She stopped herself before she blurted out the word *survive*. Quickly changed it to *thrive*. She glanced over at him and found him gazing at her intently. He was really interested in how the business did, she could tell. He wasn't simply making conversation or trying to suck up to the boss.

She liked that about him. "We're about halfway to the mine and a little ahead of schedule. How about I show you one of the greatest fishing spots in Alaska?"

"Really? Greatest?"

She chuckled. "Probably not even in the top twenty, but my grandfather loved to fish. He used to bring me and my grandmother up to this lake. We'd bring a picnic and he'd fish."

"I'd love to see it."

She felt the warmth of companionship. Knew she was falling for this guy and decided that she was okay with that. She'd make it clear to her grandmother that she wasn't attempting to repeat history, she was simply enjoying the company of a man. Who happened to be a pilot, and happened to work for Polar Air. It did not mean that Lynette had found the perfect grandson-in-law.

Claire took them off course, enjoying the sunny day and the feeling of being with the most interesting man she'd met in a long time.

"Do you ever get tired of flying?" he asked her.

She was so shocked by the question she turned to stare at him. "Tired of flying? Are you kidding? It's when I feel most alive. I look around and here I am, flying above the earth, defying gravity, seeing the glaciers and mountain peaks, the ocean and the trees from the sky. It's the most amazing thing I've ever done. I am grateful every day that I get to fly." The second she stopped speaking she felt a little embarrassed. She'd given away something very personal. If he laughed at her— She glanced over at him, and found him looking back at her not with derision but in complete agreement. "You?" she asked.

"I always think flying is like sex. No matter how

amazing a trip is, I can't wait for the next one. Every flight is different, sometimes challenging, but I get to heights I never imagined and, well, it's always a rush."

And she thought, listening to him, that she hadn't had enough good sex in her life. The thought flicked through her mind that Max might be able to change that.

"There's the lake," she said as it appeared, a silver sparkle below them.

As she took the plane lower for a closer look, a flock of geese came into view, sublimely uninterested in the fact that they were directly in front of her. She pulled up on the stick hard to get above the geese. Something she'd done many times in the past. When she tried to take the plane back down she realized she had a problem.

"The stick's not working properly. I've lost my elevator."

CLAIRE'S CALM TONE didn't fool Max. "We're still climbing," he said, which was obvious. Soon they'd reach a stall point. He didn't say what they both knew. Without the elevator they were seriously screwed.

He watched her work the throttle, back off on power. "I'm trying to time it so we stall out at the end of the lake. Near the shoreline."

Her calmness in the face of disaster was working in their favor, as was her obvious skill as a pilot. But without an elevator their chances weren't too good.

When everything worked in harmony, flying was the greatest pleasure in life. But one mechanical problem could turn a symphony into a death march.

"I'm going to try and flare out at the bottom," she said. All she could do was try and delay the inevitable. "Hang on."

For the next few minutes the plane rose and dipped while she fought for some kind of control. Sweat beaded everywhere sweat could bead. She felt the strain in her arms and the tension in her jaw where her teeth were clamped so tightly together from the effort of holding on. Without her elevator she felt like a giant, unseen hand had her plane on a string, jerking it up and then dropping it down again. Their only hope was to manipulate the inevitable stall until they were as close to the ground—or in this case the lake—as possible.

Max didn't panic and for that she was grateful. She had a moment of true regret that a pilot she'd come to like, who had worked such a short time for Polar Air, should end his life so young.

"You can do this," he said quietly, as though reading the despair in her thoughts.

She nodded, though he probably couldn't see her. The lake was their only chance.

"Lake's too calm," she said. "I can't see properly." With the lake flat calm it was difficult to differentiate the water from the sky. "I need ripples. Throw something."

He nodded. Cranked open the side window. As she turned, he grabbed cushions from the back. Chucked them out, so that when they hit the surface of the lake they'd create the definition she needed.

As they drew closer to hitting down, she said, "Okay, open your door."

Both of them pushed their doors open a little. She didn't have to explain to Max that having the doors open on impact would prevent them being trapped inside if the doors jammed. The sound of the wind rushed in.

Trees were close, like jagged green saws all pointing up, reaching for the vulnerable belly of the plane.

Her arms were trembling now with the strain. "I'm sorry, Max," she cried, as the last of the trees scraped the bottom of the aircraft and the lake came at them too fast.

They hit and the impact jerked her back and then forward. There was a sickening thud and then the thing she'd feared most. The roll as the aircraft flipped.

And began to sink.

The heavy mining equipment would drag the small plane down like an anchor. She was fuzzily aware that they were still alive and they had to get out.

"See you on the surface," she yelled.

"Roger."

She unbuckled, turned and pushed against the door with both feet as cold, frigid cold, lake water poured into the cockpit.

Fishing. Her grandfather. As she fought her way out of the plane, she reached into the pocket of the door and grabbed the fishing bag she kept there as a reminder of her grandfather, kind of a superstitious good-luck charm.

Then she oriented herself, looking for the light, and scissored her legs, fighting to reach the top. It was hard to believe that a lake could be this frigid in late summer, she thought, as she dragged her body up to the light.

She emerged, gasping from the cold. She glanced around, looking for her copilot. Where was he?

She kicked her legs, turning a full circle. "Max?" she tried to shout but she was so cold the word came out as a gasp.

He'd responded earlier when she'd called to him,

right after the crash. He hadn't sounded like he was in distress. He said he'd see her at the surface.

What if he hadn't got out?

The plane was sinking fast. Already the wheels were below the surface. She swam to where she thought Max should have surfaced, took a deep breath, prepared to dive down and then, to her intense relief, a head popped up, all dripping black hair.

"Max! You're all right."

"It's frickin' cold. Let's get out of here."

She couldn't agree more. They headed for shore, fortunately not too far away. Still, the cold, her clothing and probably the fishing bag slung over her shoulder all slowed her down.

She was tiring fast. It wasn't far to the shore but her teeth were chattering and it felt as though she were swimming through icy-cold Jell-O. Every stroke was an effort, and kicking her feet was a monumental task.

"Almost there," Max yelled to her as though he felt her distress. Probably because he shared it.

She felt herself becoming uncoordinated. Her arms and legs didn't seem to want to obey her brain.

She could see the shore of the lake but it didn't feel as though she was getting any closer. Her body felt heavy, made of lead. She was sinking, just like the plane. She coughed as her mouth filled with water.

"You can stand!" a voice yelled at her.

A hand hauled her to her feet. She stumbled, but he was right. She could stand. Max held on to her hand. Half pulled, half dragged her from the water and onto the shore. She flopped onto a sandy patch, gasping, shivering.

They were alive, which was good. But they were soaking wet and in the middle of the Alaskan wilderness. Not so good.

8

CLAIRE WAS HALF passed out on the beach, trying to get her breathing to steady and the shivering to stop.

Max crawled over and began pulling at her clothing. She tried to slap his hands away. "What are you doing?" She wanted to sound indignant, but she really didn't have the energy.

"Need to dry out our clothes while there's still some sun," he gasped.

"Right. Of course." She tried to unzip her flight jacket but he pushed her unsteady hands away. "Let me." He said it as though his only wish in life was to unzip her jacket.

She knew her thoughts were fuzzy, which couldn't be good, but she had to smile. "You are such a charmer," she muttered.

"I didn't think you'd noticed," he said, easing the jacket off her shoulders.

"Oh, I noticed."

He laid her jacket on a rocky outcrop. Weighed it down with a stone. She watched him haul his own jacket off and place it beside hers.

"Now what?" Her teeth were chattering so it was

hard to get the words out. "Do you strip us both naked and hold me close to ward off hypothermia?"

"Much as I'd like to, that's an old wives' tale. You keep a cold person warm by feeding them hot drinks and wrapping them in a sleeping bag. If you crawl in naked with them you don't raise their body temperature, they lower yours."

"Oh." She noticed he was digging into a blue nylon pack and as it sank in, her eyes widened.

"You went back for the emergency pack?" She'd have shrieked if she had the energy. "That's why it took you so long to come to the surface."

"Figured we probably needed it," he said reasonably.

She imagined taking that extra time to grab the pack even as the plane was sinking, and then having to swim to the surface. It was a miracle he'd made it. "You could have drowned."

He grinned at her. "But I didn't. And now we have an emergency pack." He dug through. "Aha! As I'd hoped." He pulled out a small silver thermal wrap.

The entire emergency kit was encased in a thick plastic bag so everything in it was dry. Including the red sleeping bag Max was deftly pulling from its stuff sack. "Well, well. Somebody really went to town. A sleeping bag! And waterproof matches and a pot." He nodded. "Good. Bottled drinking water and purification tablets."

"It doesn't weigh much and gives a person a better chance of survival."

He rolled the sleeping bag out on the soft sand. "Come on," he said.

"I can't get in there with my wet clothes on."

"True. Do you need help undressing?"

"No. Just turn your back."

"Claire."

"I'm serious."

He heaved a long-suffering sigh. Unzipped the bag and then turned his back to her. "Let me know if you need any help," he said.

"I won't." But it was more difficult than she'd imagined to strip off her wet clothes while her hands were shaking so badly. She knew it wasn't only the cold making her shake. It was also shock.

But she wasn't planning to be a damsel in distress so Max could rescue her. She'd done all right so far.

She managed to peel the wet clothes off her body. Since she couldn't put them out to dry without revealing herself to Max, she tossed her clothes in front of him. "Here."

"Thanks."

While he busied himself putting her things out on the rock, she wrapped herself in the thermal blanket and then crawled into the sleeping bag, ridiculously glad he'd retrieved the emergency kit and survived.

She watched him laying out her utilitarian shirt and pants and tried not to feel embarrassed as he placed her bra and panties alongside them. She supposed that defying death together was pretty intimate. What was a pair of panties in comparison?

Then her copilot began to strip.

She knew he was doing the sensible thing, getting his wet clothes off so they could dry on rock that held the heat of the day, giving his body a chance to dry while there was still some warmth in the sun. A good woman would turn her gaze elsewhere and give the man some privacy.

She wondered if perhaps she wasn't as good a woman as she'd imagined. Because she couldn't look away.

He was facing away from her so he couldn't know

that her gaze was fixed on him. As he peeled off his shirt she noticed his back was chiseled with muscle. His shoulders made it look as though he spent half his life in the swimming pool and the other half in the gym, which she knew wasn't true. But wow, the guy was cut.

He laid his shirt on the warm rock and then reached for his belt buckle. She felt as though her eyes were stuck in place. She couldn't seem to force herself to look away. He peeled the wet pants down his hips and revealed wet boxer shorts that didn't hide much. His hips were lean, his butt tight and round. His legs were slightly bowed but all muscle.

The sleeping bag was warming her nicely. Watching Max remove his clothes was doing the rest of the job.

MAX KEPT A careful eye on Claire but she warmed up quickly once she was inside the sleeping bag. The heat of the day was already passing, but at least they still had hours of sunshine and the forecast called for dry weather for the next few days.

That was working in their favor. He suspected not a lot of other factors were.

"When will the mine be letting Polar Air know that we didn't make it?"

"Couple of hours from now, I imagine." Claire wasn't shivering anymore, he was relieved to see. He'd stripped down to his boxers, figuring modesty had to give way to safety and if the fact that he was nearly naked bothered her, she hadn't mentioned it.

He nodded. Gazed up at the sky, so clear and blue. "Any chance another plane will happen by?"

"Probably not."

"And the ELT is at the bottom of the lake." He stared

at the calm surface. No sign of the plane. "How deep is it?"

"I don't know for sure, but the lakes tend to be very deep around here. I doubt the signal will get picked up."

"So, basically, we're on our own."

"Basically." She blew out a breath. "I went off course. Didn't radio Lynette to let her know. That was stupid."

"Yeah, but the detour probably saved our lives."

"I know." She hadn't wanted to dwell on their narrow escape. It was still too fresh. And too narrow. But he was right, of course. The direct route to the mine was nothing but trees and mountain. The chances of them surviving that crash had they stuck to the planned route would have been pretty much zero.

"The detour and you being a damned fine pilot," he said.

She smiled briefly.

"And I watched you fight that throttle. Not for a second did you lose your cool. I owe you my life."

"Does this mean you won't sue Polar Air for almost killing you?" She was only half joking.

He stared across at her, a troubled expression on his face. "It wasn't Polar Air who tried to kill us."

"What do you mean?"

"Come on. We both checked that plane this morning. There is no way that elevator should have gone."

"You can't be suggesting—" She couldn't finish the sentence. The possibility he seemed to be floating was unthinkable.

"Suggesting that the aircraft was sabotaged?" He finished the thought anyway. "That is exactly what I mean. When you went up, the elevator suddenly jammed. Same thing would have happened if you'd tried to land. I bet he put something in there that wouldn't jam the equipment until you were in flight. So your flight check would show everything working."

The possibility appalled her. "But who would do such a thing?"

"Gee, I don't know. Got any former employees with a grudge? Somebody who stole a lot of money they can't pay back? Somebody who knows the fleet as well as you do?"

"You can't be suggesting Frank Carmondy would try and kill us."

"He gets my vote."

"No," she said. Then she shook her head and gazed out at the lake where her plane now rested in its watery grave. Where she and Max had so nearly ended up. "Oh, no."

"He came to see you yesterday."

She nodded. "But he wanted to let me know that he's in AA. That he's mortgaging his house to pay us back." She swallowed. "He even brought a photograph that he had of me and my grandmother and grandfather and him back when I first became a pilot."

Max didn't seem very impressed. "He could tell you anything. If he planned to make sure you disappeared, who cared what he told you?"

"But—"

"Did he by any chance ask you not to tell anyone about your little meeting?"

"No." She thought back. "Not exactly. He simply asked me to give him a few days to get his financing in place and we'd meet again."

"Knowing there'd never be a meeting."

"But there's still Lynette. She knows most of it. He can't kill her as well. It would be too obvious." She gulped as a sudden spasm of fear for her beloved grand-mother shook her. "Could he?"

"I don't think he'll need to. Think about it. It was you who decided to go after him. If Lynette's grieving over you, she's not going to have the energy or desire for an unpleasant lawsuit. My guess is she'd sell up and move into town."

"She'll be devastated." She didn't want to believe what Max was suggesting even though, on some level, she knew she'd harbored the same suspicion. "I still can't believe it. How would he even know we were coming here? I didn't exactly discuss flight operations with him."

"Did you ever step out of the office during your meeting and leave him alone?"

Had she? She thought back to the meeting with Frank. Tried to recall their conversation. Had they been interrupted? "Yes," she said, thinking back. "Arnie came in and I left Frank in the office for a few minutes."

"Plenty of time for him to check your schedule."

"He had no way of knowing you'd be with me."

"No," he said. "He couldn't have known. He probably hoped you'd be alone. I'd have been collateral damage."

"Oh, Max," she said, holding her hand out. "I'm so sorry I almost got you killed."

He reached out and gripped her hand. She liked the feeling of his fingers entwined with hers. "You didn't almost kill me. You saved both our lives." His grip tightened. "We're going to be okay."

"Then we better figure out how to get back there before Lynette has a chance to get too worried."

"I know. When the office gets word that we didn't make it, and they can't contact us, they'll start searching. Trouble is, they'll search the wrong area."

"Let's give it a few hours. You know the first rule of a crash. Don't leave the plane."

He nodded. "If the ELT's working we should be out of here in a few hours."

"Right." Her thermal blanket crinkled when she moved. "And if that signal's not being picked up, then we need to hike out."

"How long will it take?"

"About two days, I think." She pulled up a mental map of the area. "If we head due west we should hit a logging road. We can follow it down to the main highway."

"Seems like a plane would be easier to find than two people on a logging road."

"Yeah. And this is a good spot. Fish in the lake, water, there are water purification tablets in the emergency pack, right?"

"Yep. Also bug repellent, a compass, first-aid kit, basic provisions and a flare gun."

"We'll stay here for the night. If they don't find us by morning, we should hike out."

The conversation had left her feeling sick with the horror that a man their family had trusted might have tried to kill her and Max.

Was it possible? Had Frank, their family friend, sabotaged their aircraft?

She shivered and snuggled deeper into the sleeping bag.

9

MAX HAD THE bag of fishing tackle spread out, pleased to see that it was in good repair. Claire had already assured him that there would be fish in this lake, so they wouldn't be stuck with the few power bars and emergency rations in the pack.

A sudden chuckle from his companion caused him to glance her way. "What?"

"I was just thinking, if you say flying is like sex, today you experienced flightus interruptus."

He felt her amusement as her body made the sleeping bag quake.

"You know what you were saying about hypothermia and sharing a sleeping bag?"

"Sure. Old wives' tale."

"Well, the thing is, there is only the one sleeping bag."

He appeared to think about it carefully. Glanced around as though there might be other options. But, of course, there were plenty of thick trees, some rocks, gallons of lake. But alternative places to sleep? Not so much.

She watched him work out that she was right. Glanced

at her with a rueful expression. "I've been longing to get you into bed from the second I set eyes on you. But not like this."

"Really?"

They'd nearly died together so what was the big deal if the conversation got intimate? "The first time I saw you? I walk into Polar Air's office, for my scheduled interview with Frank Carmondy. I'm focused on what I'm going to say, making a good impression. I open the door and the first thing I see is the shapeliest ass I've ever come across, snugged nicely into a pair of tight jeans. I was still checking you out when you fired Frank."

She chuckled. "I was so busy telling him off that I didn't even hear you come in. Well, if we're being honest, I noticed your eyes right away, and then your buff body."

"And now, here we are. Half-naked and definitely spending the night together."

"I know what you mean. Normally, if I was going to spend the night with you, I'd put on my best underwear." She settled into the down bag, in her oh-so-practical cotton briefs, the bra that was built for utility not sexiness and the socks that she wasn't entirely sure matched. At least they'd dried enough that she could put them back on. "I'd have bathed and done my hair." She smiled at her own routine. "I have this special body lotion that makes me feel sexy. You wouldn't know it, but if I was wearing it that would be a sign that I was, you know, interested."

He turned to her. "What does this lotion smell like?"

She raised her brows. "You want me to give away my secrets?"

"I want to make sure I don't miss any signals you might give out. Hypothetically."

"Well, hypothetically, assuming I was interested in spending the night with you in a sexual way, the lotion I'd put on smells like rosewater and almonds."

"This is very confusing to me. I'm not sure what rosewater smells like. Does it smell like roses?"

"Yeah. Basically." She shifted and the bag rustled. "And almonds."

"Roses and almonds. Glad you warned me. I doubt I'd have picked up on that as a big sex signal."

"I think I do that one more for me. The lotion makes me feel sexy. And it's very moisturizing."

He settled himself on a nearby log. "Let's say you were sending signals that were definitely for me and not just something that makes you feel good in your skin. What might those be?"

"You want me to give away my signals? Don't you think you should have to work for this at all? I don't want to make getting me into bed too easy for you."

"But women always think men are so much more perceptive than we really are. Honestly, a lot of those so-called signals you think you're sending out never get picked up on."

"You mean you don't notice?"

"I mean, we're simple creatures. We like simple, clear communication."

"Like what?"

"Like, 'I feel like having sex with you right now.'"

She laughed out loud. "That is so pathetic. No self-respecting woman would ever say that to a man she wasn't already involved with. And, even then, I doubt she'd be so blunt."

"Why not?"

She thought about it. "Because we like to be wooed. Well, I guess I can't speak for other women. I like to be wooed. I want a man to put some effort into making me want him."

"But don't you think you should meet him halfway? No guy wants to put himself out there with a woman only to be rejected."

"Yes. That's what I'm saying. That's why we send out signals. Little things that show we're interested, so you know that you're not wasting your time." She huffed out a breath. "Think about it from our point of view. No woman wants to be in a position where she ends up turning a nice man down. So we send signals that say we're interested and signals to indicate that we're not."

"You know that's like a dictionary in a foreign language."

"No, it isn't. Body language is universal."

"Okay. Give me some of your 'yes, I'm interested' signals."

"What, now?"

"Why not?"

She barely knew where to begin. "Because my hair is hanging in my face like wet laundry. My clothes are hanging over on that rock like, well, wet laundry. I'm chilled, hungry and a little bit scared."

"First, you look great. To me, you always look great." He considered the rest of her statement. "I don't care what you're wearing. You should be warming up by now. I'll get a fire on. Hungry? We'll have tons of fish for dinner. So long as we stay near this lake there will be food. As for scared, yeah, I get that. But we made it to the ground alive and unharmed. That is a freakin' miracle. Now it's simply a matter of getting to a place where we can be picked up." He grinned at her. "Think of it as a wilderness adventure. People pay big bucks to fly into remote areas and hike."

She groaned. "If I had to be stranded in the middle of nowhere, did I have to get Mr. Optimist as a companion?"

"What do you want? Somebody who's going to remind you of how bad things are? Hey, I'm not suggesting this is the greatest day of my life, but compared to how I thought it was going to end a few hours ago? I'm pretty damned happy to be right here."

"You're right, of course."

"And you were smart enough to grab your grandpa's tackle box."

"And, even though it scared the hell out of me at the time, I'm glad you managed to snag that emergency pack."

"So we're good then. And we can go back to talking about sex."

"We weren't talking about sex!"

"See? That's exactly what I mean about women. If you're describing the body lotion you put on when you want to entice a man into your bed then I think we're talking about sex. What do you think we're talking about?"

"I think I'm so happy to still be alive that I don't really know what I'm talking about."

He nodded. "I get that. And as much as I'd like to sit around talking about sex all day, I think somebody better go catch dinner."

"Sure. Can you fish?"

"I'm not bad. Not as good as my buddy Adam. We call him the fish whisperer. It's like they want to come to him."

"I'd like to meet your friends sometime."

"I once took a wilderness course, one of those ones where they leave you out in the middle of nowhere for a couple of days and you have to live off the land. It was an amazing experience."

"Kind of like now," she said.

"Except now, we have fishing tackle." Deftly, he put together a line, baiting it with a piece of an energy bar from the emergency stash.

"Not a bad catch," he said sometime later, surveying three fish, freshly caught and glistening in the late-afternoon sun.

"Not bad at all," she agreed.

They gathered firewood together, searching for small dry twigs and grass to get the flames started and then some larger pieces to sustain the blaze.

"You want to clean the fish or start the fire?" he asked.

"I'll start the fire."

He grinned at her, but didn't say anything, simply hauled out a knife from the bag of fishing gear and went to work. He used the same knife to whittle a spearlike end onto a thin alder branch, threaded the cleaned fish onto it and roasted the filets over the coals.

They ate their fish sitting by the fire. It was tasty and she was grateful to have hot food. Still, she found herself saying, "A squeeze of fresh lemon would be nice."

"Oh, yeah," he said, pushing a piece of fish into his mouth with his fingertips. Somehow he even managed to make eating with his hands look elegant. "And a nice crisp white wine."

"Maybe with some seasoned rice."

"And lightly steamed asparagus."

"Oh, and bread," she sighed, pushing more fish into

her own mouth. "I love bread. I wish the whole world wasn't on some diet or other that shuns the stuff. Wheat Belly, Atkins, they all go after poor, humble bread."

"I agree. I love bread. My mom used to make her own. I love it hot, fresh out of the oven and dripping with butter."

"Oh," she moaned. "I want to meet your mom. I might want to move in with her."

His eyes glinted as he stared at her across the fire. "Who knows? Maybe one day you will meet her."

"I hope so." And she realized, as she said the words, that she didn't mean them in an "if we get out of here alive" sort of way. She really did want to meet his mother. A woman who made bread from scratch. Imagine.

"My mother died when I was a teenager but I still remember her pretty well. She wasn't very domestic. And of course Grandma was too busy flying planes and running a business. We ate a lot of simple meals. Barbecues in the summer. Pasta and one-dish casseroles in the winter." She shrugged. "I turned out to be like her. I hate wasting time in the kitchen. I'd rather be outside."

"I am a great cook," Max informed her with simple pride. "My mother insisted my sister and I both learn. I loved it."

"Really?" It wasn't that hard to imagine Max in a stainless-steel kitchen concocting complicated recipes. He almost looked like one of those cute young chefs who get their own TV shows. "What are your specialties?"

"When we get home, I am going to cook you a South American feast. We begin with *seviche*. My special recipe. Then for the main course, I think *lomo asado*, which is basically steak but, as you know, there is an art to everything. For dessert, there will be—" He stopped himself. "No. I think dessert will be a surprise."

He was always surprising her, she thought. "You know, I don't normally date people I work with."

"I believe you've mentioned it."

She bit into a fish bone and removed it as delicately as she could. "I think when you've been in a crash with someone, you can make an exception."

"I agree. There should be."

"Okay, then."

"Okay, you'll agree to date me?"

"Okay, I'll agree to let you cook me a wonderful dinner. The rest might depend on how good your dessert is."

He chuckled softly. "Oh, I promise you'll enjoy it," he said in a way that suggested he wasn't talking about food anymore.

She felt a quiver of response deep in her belly. Perhaps it was the adrenaline still affecting her, but something about the near-death experience had sure reminded her that she was a woman in her prime. That she was a vital, sexual being who had needs.

And Max seemed like the kind of man who could meet her needs extremely well.

She shifted.

He noticed immediately. "Are you cold?"

"No. Just trying to get comfortable."

He put more wood on the fire and the flames danced up against the deepening twilight surrounding them. She kept her focus on the fire and on Max and tried not to notice that they were surrounded by seemingly impenetrable forest. A few stars were out above them, but the moon was nothing but a sliver. She was ridiculously glad to have company. It was only at the last minute she'd asked him to come along. Normally, she'd do this trip alone. She believed she was strong enough and resourceful enough that she could have survived a few days and hiked out alone if necessary. But she was glad she didn't have to.

"I was thinking," he said, "that we should take turns sleeping. There's only one bag and the other can keep watch."

She nodded. She'd been thinking the same thing. There were plenty of bears in the area, both black bears and grizzlies, wolves—though in her experience the timber wolves were shy creatures who mainly kept to themselves—and mountain lions. It was probably a good idea to keep the fire going and an ear cocked.

"Shall I take the first watch?"

"Sure."

They stoked up the fire. He went to the lake's edge and she heard water splashing. He was clearly washing himself, probably doing his best to keep up his level of fastidious cleanliness.

When he returned, he slipped into the sleeping bag. "Wake me in four hours. Unless you need me."

"I will."

She could see the dark sausage shape of the bag with Max inside it. He didn't thrash or turn and seemed to be asleep in minutes.

She kept herself awake by stoking the fire and by trying to imagine what could have gone wrong with the plane. The August night grew cool, even though she was sitting as near the fire as she dared.

She heard the scurrying of nocturnal creatures, the whisper of bats passing, the quiet lap of the lake when the breeze picked up. But other than that, the night was quiet and still.

She never did wake him up. As she gazed into the fire, wishing Max had never put thoughts of sabotage into her head, even though she realized that he had reason for his suspicion, Max spoke.

"Are you cold?"

"Not really. Go back to sleep. You've got some time yet."

But he was already crawling out of the sleeping bag. "I feel wide-awake. I'll start my watch now. You get some sleep."

"But—"

"If you argue, the warmth will dissipate from the bag. Get in now while it's still holding my body heat."

Knowing it was stupid to argue, and realizing that the shock and trauma of the day had taken their toll, she rose. Stretched out her cramped back and headed to the sleeping area.

He held the bag open for her, as though he were holding the door open as he escorted her to a restaurant.

"Thank you," she said, slipping into the bag that was, as he'd promised, still warm. She snuggled down into the softness, hardly noticing the hard ground beneath her.

"Sleep well," he said, stroking her hair. The gesture was both comforting and somehow sexy.

She was thinking how glad she was that he was here when it suddenly dawned on her that it was because of him they'd altered course and crashed, not into dense forest and mountain, but into a relatively small lake.

The detour had saved them.

Which meant that in a strange way, Max had saved her life.

10

WHEN SHE AWOKE, the sun was already up. She blinked and stretched, realizing that she was stiff and bruised from the aftereffects of the crash.

Max was fishing.

As she approached him he put a finger to his lips and pointed. To their right, partway up the shore, she saw a shadowy figure that she thought at first was a dog. Then realized how foolish she was being. Where would a dog come from?

It was a wolf. Rangy and long-limbed. Not a lone wolf, either. Behind it she saw more soft canine shadows ambling along the waterfront. She sensed they were fully alert to her and Max's presence, watching the two humans as carefully as they were being watched.

There were six wolves in the pack. They tracked the shoreline and then disappeared into the bush. "Must be their regular route," she said softly when the last wolf had melted into the trees.

"Or we scared them out of their usual routine," Max suggested.

"I bet they don't see many humans." She yawned. "Oh, I would kill for coffee."

"I can't do coffee, but I boiled some water. Think dark thoughts while you drink it."

She'd never paid as much attention to the emergency pack as she should have, but she was unbelievably grateful to have it now. There was a one-burner wilderness camping stove, a single pot, a few nutrition bars and water purification drops. Waterproof matches, some rope, a compass and flares. Which they would shoot off if they heard a plane approaching.

She laughed. "That's not difficult to do. If the signal from the ELT was getting picked up we'd be out of here by now. We've got to hike two full days to get to the road."

"Maybe a rescue plane will spot us."

"Maybe."

She drank a little water. Disappeared behind a rock and discreetly washed herself. Feeling much more human, she put her clothes back on and filled the makeshift pot with bright orange salmon berries from a patch she found growing.

"Fruit for breakfast," she announced when she returned to where Max was once more grilling fish.

"That's a lot of fish," she said when she saw that he had four hanging from a stick and four more cleaned and ready for cooking.

"I don't know when we'll next find a food source. We can bring the extra fish along with us for later."

"Good thinking."

She shared out the berries and they ate quickly. The sun was up and the day would soon grow hot. They needed to get moving.

It didn't take long to pack up their camp, since they didn't have much of anything with them. After they both covered any exposed skin with liberal amounts of insect repellent, Max insisted on taking the pack.

There weren't many options as far as which direction they would hike in. She knew the area pretty well and if they went due west they'd come to a logging road. "We can follow that down to the main highway."

The difficulty was going to be getting to the logging road. The forest was dense. They'd have to follow animal trails which were notoriously random. And, of course, they were likely to come across the animals that used those trails. The area was rich with black bears and, as Claire often told the tourists she transported, Alaska was home to one of the largest populations of grizzly bears, numbering around 30,000. The average male grew seven feet tall and weighed in at around 500 pounds. It was great patter when you were looking down at their habitat from the sky. Now she wished she didn't know quite so much about bears. She did not want to bump into a hungry grizzly.

They set out due west and the going was tough. Branches, vines and thorns scratched at their skin and hair. The path was lumpy with roots and rocks and patches of mud.

They equipped themselves with sturdy branches that functioned both as walking sticks and as protection in case they encountered dangerous wildlife, though the most aggressive creatures seemed to be airborne. In spite of the bug repellent, the mosquitoes were a torment.

Grimly, they pressed on. Mile after mile of twisting trail that sometimes petered out or branched into several paths, any one of which might lead somewhere or nowhere.

Although they both wore sturdy boots, they weren't

properly equipped for hiking and they knew it. They shared the water in the emergency pack, trying to eke it out until they found another water source.

Trees that had fallen across the trails had to be clambered over or squeezed under. It was strenuous going.

They snacked on berries along the way and stopped around noon to eat some of their fish.

At one point in the early afternoon, they emerged from the deep woods to an open patch of ground and startled a sleeping snake so it slithered away.

Two hours later, they stumbled upon a bear. It was a big black bear. A full-grown male. Fortunately, not a female with cubs to protect, but a black bear is a beast to be treated with respect.

The animal was happily munching on a patch of wild blackberries, reaching up on its hind legs to reach the big juicy ones high up.

If she'd been watching the berry feast on a documentary program, Claire would have been charmed. But the problem was, the big bear was blocking the path. She didn't think pushing past him and saying "excuse me" was going to work.

Going back the way they'd come was futile.

In the end, they simply waited. He showed no interest in them. He wanted his berries.

For more than an hour they waited while the bear munched his food and the mosquitoes and the odd bee buzzed. At least they could rest from their relentless walking, but they had no idea when he'd stop eating. And even then, what would they do if he turned their way?

Finally, the bear dropped back to his four paws, swung his head their way for a heart-stopping ten seconds and then ambled away in the opposite direction.

They heard crashing of undergrowth and waited five more minutes before venturing along the same path.

"At least he left a few for us," Max said cheerfully as he popped a plump blackberry into her mouth. It was warm from the sun and bursting with flavor.

She was tired, her feet hurt, she itched all over from mosquito bites, and worry that some catastrophe would befall them before they reached the logging road plagued her. But Max had a way of making things seem better than they were. So, she munched her berry and was thankful for the burst of sweetness on her tongue.

BY LATE AFTERNOON, she felt as though she couldn't walk one more step.

Max never asked her how she felt.

He didn't offer her sympathy or urge her on.

Instead, he told her stories.

Stories about his childhood. Silly pranks he and his sister had played on each other. Stories about him and his two best friends, Dylan and Adam.

"We did everything together. Little League, Boy Scouts, team sports when we got older.

"We still play hockey together," he said. "You'll have to meet them one of these days."

"I'd like to." She wondered if word had leaked out that they were missing. If his friends knew. But Max didn't bring that up.

He told her about his friend Adam. "Adam has the first birthday out of the three of us. When he turned thirty-five, his parents threw a party for him. And June, his mom, surprised the hell out of him when she showed a video of his fifth birthday." He grinned at the memory, whacking some low-growing branches out of the way so they could pass, as though his sturdy stick was a machete. It was exhausting work but he didn't seem to notice.

"She asked the three of us what we were going to be when we grew up. The amazing thing is, we all ended up doing what we said we would." He whacked another patch of heavy green. "Or pretty close, anyway."

They were aiming for a river tributary that would cross their path. That, she calculated, would be close to halfway to the road.

"Then she asked us who we were going to marry." A dark line of sweat down his back was the only evidence he was putting any effort into this hike. "We were five. But we all had answers. Adam was going to marry Princess Diana. Remember, this was 1983. And Dylan planned to marry Xena, the comic book character." He shook his head. "Boys. Knowing Dylan he still wants to marry Xena."

"How about you?"

"I was always more sensible than the others. I said I wasn't getting married until I was grown up."

"And have you?"

"Married?" His tone provided the answer. "No."

"Maybe that means you haven't grown up yet."

He chuckled. "Oh, yeah. You want to know how immature me and my buddies are? We ended up making a bet the night of Adam's party. All of us were determined to be the last bachelor standing."

"Last bachelor standing? This is something to be proud of?"

"That was a long night. Scotch may have been involved."

"I thought you said your friend Adam was getting married?"

"He is." He turned back to her and his teeth gleamed white. "One down, one to go."

It sounded to her like a singularly foolish bet and annoyed her on some level. "And what do you win?"

"Win?"

"Does this foolish bet include a prize?"

He turned once more to look at her. A sheen of sweat gleamed on his forehead, otherwise he looked as cool as a bowl of ice cream. "Prize?" He seemed to think about it for a moment. "Bragging rights, I guess."

She could feel a hot spot forming on her heel. She hoped there were blister pads or some kind of plaster in the first-aid kit. "It sounds to me as though Adam is the person who really won your bet."

"Yep. That's exactly what Adam says."

Well, at least one of them had some sense, she thought as she trudged on.

Was she seriously considering dating a man who would enter a contest where not getting married was the goal?

She watched him moving through the forest, his shoulder muscles rippling as he beat back the branches and vines, his body moving with athletic grace. Even through her fatigue she felt a quiver of desire.

What did it matter? She wasn't looking for anything permanent. She could have some fun with Max knowing he wouldn't suddenly go all serious on her.

It was a perfect arrangement. He'd proven himself to be a good pilot, a good man to have around in an emergency. She enjoyed his company, was attracted to him physically. Something about him suggested that he wasn't going to make a thirty-year career out of his job at Polar Air. They'd probably keep him until the snow fell. If he couldn't handle an Alaskan winter, he'd move on. And even if he did she doubted he'd last more than a year. She could enjoy him while he was here and they'd part friends.

So why did she feel so irritated by that stupid bet?

11

CLAIRE WAS BEGINNING to think they'd never hit water, that, somehow, in spite of the compass, they'd been wandering in circles, going nowhere.

And then, they heard the blessed sound of water. It felt as though they burst out of the trees and there was the river, swift, blue and as welcome to her as the sun in the morning.

With a cry of relief, she ran to the edge of the river and knelt down, plunging her hands into the cold water, splashing it on her face, and then, using her cupped hands, she drank and drank until she could drink no more. She couldn't imagine waiting to purify the water and at the rate it was racing, she doubted there was any need to.

Water had never tasted so good. Even the most expensive champagne she'd ever sipped, and admittedly she'd never sampled the really top-drawer stuff, didn't come close. She glanced down river and saw that Max was sucking back cold, clear water as greedily as she was. Clean, tidy Max glanced up at her and grinned, water running down his chin. For a second their gazes held and she felt a surge of sexual heat so strong she caught her breath.

He rose, never letting his gaze drop, and she felt powerless to break the connection. He came closer, not even bothering to wipe the water off his face so it caught in the late-afternoon sun and sparkled.

Closer.

Never breaking stride until he stood right in front of her, so close she could see the stubble on his face and glimpse the black flecks in his dark brown eyes. Eyes that stared at her with an intensity that made her shiver.

He moved even closer. She didn't step back but held her ground, held his gaze.

He grabbed her shoulders, pulled her to him and kissed her with the same urgency as when he'd drunk deep of the stream only moments ago.

She felt the roughness of a face that hadn't seen a razor in two days, the coldness of the river water on his lips, the hot, potent energy flowing through him and into her.

She wanted more. More of that energy, more of his solid sexiness, more of the feeling that something positive and wonderful was happening in the midst of this madness.

She pulled him closer and he responded by deepening the kiss. She felt the warmth of the sun on her shoulders, heard the buzz of insects and the rush of water. Sensed the powerful attraction between them as his tongue took mastery of her mouth.

She'd known kisses before, of course. Friendly kisses, exploratory kisses, passionate kisses, but she had never experienced a kiss that seemed to lift her off her feet and transport her to a different place. She had never known a kiss that made her body feel like it was buzzing with excitement. She couldn't stand still; she found herself squirming with desire, wanting him as she'd never wanted a man. She knew, with an instinct she didn't question, that it was the same for him. Like a quiet but insistent *yes* dancing along their nerve endings pulling them ever and inevitably closer.

He pulled back and they were both panting. "Wow," he said.

"I thought we were going to have a date when we got back?" she reminded him.

"We are going to have a date. We are going to have the date to end all dates." He drew in a sharp breath. "Does it matter to you?"

The thought of waiting until they were back in civilization, until there was an evening in both their schedules that they could devote to romance, was no sooner contemplated than dropped. She knew on some level that this crazy life-or-death adventure was causing her to throw caution to the winds, but she realized she didn't want her caution back. Let it stay floating on wind currents, like an aircraft headed through a weather system. For now, she needed that man with every fiber of her being. She'd worry about consequences later.

She answered his question by putting her arms around his neck and pulling him back to her, kissing him with the same fervent desire he'd shown her. He made a small sound, half growl, half groan and pulled her even closer.

The world receded. Time stopped. Her senses were so focused on that kiss she'd have sworn the river ceased flowing and fell into silence.

He tugged at her shirt, pulling it from her pants, undoing buttons with haste. She suspected he might have ripped the thing off her, let the buttons fly where they might, except that they both knew she had only the one shirt. So he was careful. But fast.

She felt the sun on her naked shoulders, then his lips were there.

He had her bra unfastened almost faster than she could have done it herself. This man was smooth. She was sure he'd been with countless women. But when he slipped the bra off her shoulders and the sun tingled on her breasts, she felt for a moment like the first woman he'd ever seen. His gaze was worshipful and he reached for her slowly, touching her gently but firmly until her nipples ached with need. When he lowered his head and put his mouth on the tip of her breast she felt sensation spiral through her, coming to rest heavy in her belly.

She dragged at his shirt, trying to be as smooth as he'd been when he unbuttoned hers, but it was hopeless. She was too frantic. She fumbled and cursed in her haste until he laughed and stripped it off himself.

He was magnificent. Tawny and muscular and with a six-pack on him that made her want to run her tongue over the ridges of muscle in his belly.

In unspoken agreement, they finished stripping themselves, both driven by need rather than a desire for slow seduction. There was a time for slow seduction, and Claire was a sucker for it. But not here. Not today.

Today she needed to feel Max pounding within her almost as much as she'd needed that water.

She dragged off her boots and socks, then removed her pants and panties together in one lumpy movement. She was so eager to see Max that she turned at the very moment he did.

"Oh, you are so beautiful," he said. "Better than I imagined."

And he was exactly as beautiful as she'd imagined.

The powerful body of a warrior, the intelligent face of a deep thinker and a big, hard cock that seemed to her fevered imagination to be reaching for her, as though as eager to stroke her secret places as she was to feel him there.

Max ran his hands down her back, over her hips, then hoisted her up so she squeaked. He settled her on a rock ledge and stepped between her legs. Already she was panting with need.

Normally she'd have "the conversation" about testing and histories and so on before things ever got to this stage. But there was nothing normal about this. She tried to bring a little sanity to the proceeding even as her body cried out for fulfillment. "Do you have anything?" she gasped.

A flicker of wry amusement twisted his mouth. "I'm not a sixteen-year-old who carries a condom in his wallet."

"Is there anything I need to worry about?"

He shook his head. "Clean as a whistle."

Her legs were splayed and she could feel her own wetness gathering. He put a finger there and rubbed softly, finding her hot button and massaging her as though he'd been born to pleasure her. He didn't ask, but she felt she should let him know. "Me, too. No health issues."

He nodded. "Do we need to worry about getting you pregnant?"

It was hard to think with the waves of urgent desire that were building within her. She was on the pill but normally she'd insist on a condom until she knew a man better and trusted him completely. Instinctively she did trust Max, however. "No," she panted.

He must have felt how close she was, because he replaced his fingers with his cock, rubbing the tip against her most sensitive place. The different sensation, the feel of that wonderful, hot, hard man that she wanted so badly inside her was too much. Her hips began to gyrate to his rhythm. She lifted her hips up, supporting herself on her hands so she could dance with him without scraping her sensitive skin on the rock beneath her.

"Oh," she cried. He kissed her, licking deep into her mouth as she cried out her climax.

"Oh, that's right," he crooned. "That's good."

She couldn't form words. She could only mime what she needed. She nudged him with her hips, shifting until his cock was grazing the soft, swollen opening to her body. She was pulsing, wet, and felt her body begin to suck him right into her.

It was his turn to lose his mind. She saw his eyes lose their focus, then his movements became less controlled. He stroked her all the way in, all the way out, until he couldn't anymore and, grabbing her hips, began to thrust in and out of her. She felt him as deep inside her as she'd ever felt anyone. It was glorious to be stretched and stroked. There were crazy sounds coming out of her mouth, out of his. She felt her need build again. Could feel her body tightening around him. He could obviously feel it, too, because he began to tremble. She gripped his biceps and found them slick with sweat, rigid as he held her up, tried to hold himself in check.

"Let go," she cried, needing him to give her everything he had.

"Don't want to hurt you," he muttered.

"You won't."

It was all the encouragement he needed. She felt the moment he let his control snap. He thrust into her, hard and desperate, again and again, driving her up higher until she crested the peak once more and her head fell back as she cried out.

A moment later, his own cry echoed hers.

She felt the wetness gush inside her. Felt his twitch and still he moved in and out of her. More slowly now, bringing them both down easily. She felt the aftershocks, rode them as he continued pumping in and out of her. Her sighs grew more gentle and then he reached for her and kissed her with a slow sweetness that melted her heart.

"That was am—" he began.

"Mmm," she said, kissing him, cutting him off because the experience had been so superlative she didn't want words to spoil it.

He set her down and as her feet touched the ground the gravel provided a rough reminder that they were outdoors.

"I don't care how cold that river is," she said. "I am going in."

"Clean freak."

She glanced at him. Raised one eyebrow. "Are you going to watch from shore?"

He grinned, knowing he was caught. "Hell, no. I'm going in, too."

It wasn't a long dip. The cold water stole her breath, but she could at least feel a little cleaner and soothe her hot, aching feet.

Knowing she couldn't risk wet socks, she sadly left hers on the bank, but she was certain her panties would dry. She washed them as best she could and laid them out on a warm stone in the sun.

She even dunked her head, longing for shampoo. At least she could soak out the sweat and dirt.

She came out of the water shivering and lay naked

on the rock ledge, soaking in the warmth of the sun. The insects blessedly stayed away thanks to the breeze.

Max crawled up beside her naked and cold. She felt the heat of the rock beneath her, the warmth of the sun on her front and Max warming up beside her. Then heat began to kindle inside of her.

She knew he felt it, too, when his hand began to roam lazily over her body, touching her breasts, her belly and then lower.

She couldn't believe she was ready again. Two explosive orgasms and her body was still greedy for more.

A shadow fell across her face and she opened her eyes to find Max leaning over her. He kissed her mouth even as his fingers began to play between her legs.

She let her own fingers explore. His face, his warm, muscular chest, the athlete's belly and finally, his impressively hard cock.

She stroked him, squeezed him, toyed with him as he was toying with her. She cupped her hand under his balls and squeezed gently.

He began to kiss his way down her body. Even though there was no one to watch them but the odd overflying eagle, she still felt absurdly exposed. Then, as he parted her thighs and lowered his head, she stopped thinking at all.

He licked her, taking his time, building her up slowly. Then, when her hips began to gyrate, he pushed two fingers inside her and stroked to her rhythm. It was exquisite. She wanted to make this last forever but she could feel herself growing closer.

He stayed with her, keeping a steady rhythm and pressure of his tongue on her clit until she felt herself beginning to melt. He pressed on her G-spot and simultaneously sucked her clit into his mouth.

She exploded with a wild, frenzied cry. Her body

clenched against his fingers, against his tongue and he continued stroking inside her, letting her down slowly.

The roar of the river, the feel of his lips kissing his way back up her body, the wonderful pulses of remembered pleasure, all filled her with the most incredible sensation.

She'd nearly died yesterday.

And today, she'd never felt more alive.

12

THEY DINED ON fish and berries again.

"We are so lucky to be stuck out here when food is plentiful," she said.

He nodded. "And the weather's good."

She shuddered at the thought of everything that could have gone wrong, from injuries to bad weather. As though reading her mind he said, "We'd have made it, you know. In any season. We'd have survived."

"In winter?"

"Sure. Haven't you ever built a snow cave?"

She looked at him in fascination. "Have you?"

"Absolutely. Excellent skill to have." He tossed a fish bone into the fast-flowing river. "Once, my buddies Dylan and Adam and I took a winter survival course. It was pretty cool. You really get to know what you're made of."

"Did you enjoy it?"

He glanced over at her. "I'm enjoying this wilderness adventure a whole lot more. Company's better." He glanced back in the direction of the crash site. "And maybe it's more exciting because it's real."

The fire was crackling, the stars were just coming

out and she felt a quick spurt of pleasure to be here, now, with this man. She knew that tomorrow would bring rescue and all her old problems would be back on her shoulders, along with the much more sinister dilemma of what to do about Frank Carmondy. Could he really be behind the crash?

And, if so, how would they ever prove it?

Once more they took turns keeping watch and sleeping. When Claire woke she felt as though she'd been beaten up. Her back was sore from sleeping on the hard ground, her feet did not want to go back on the road and yet there was such beauty all around her. The river tumbled by, the cool air was fresh and bracing and birds were singing their hearts out.

As he had the morning before, Max had water already heating. "We're going to have to make some additions to that emergency pack," she said, as she accepted the pot and sipped hot water. "We need those little packets of espresso coffee. And some mugs."

"Here, have a power bar." She took the bar and peeled open the packaging. The bar was dense and chewy and she sincerely hoped it was packed with energy.

"Hey, don't look so glum," Mr. Cheerful in the Morning said. "We're going home today."

She felt anxiety clutch at her chest. She hoped her memory was correct and they were headed for a logging road that would lead them to an emergency phone or a larger road. There was a lot more wilderness out here than there was civilization. But she knew this state, she reminded herself. She'd flown all over it. They'd find their way out.

They would.

So, she forced a smile and said, "When we get home I am planning to shower for at least an hour."

"I'm going straight for food."

They packed swiftly and put out the fire.

Next they had to figure out how to get across the river.

"How deep do you think it is?" she asked Max, raising her voice so he could hear her over the rushing water, though of course he'd have no more idea than she did.

"Hard to say. And the current's swift." He scanned the riverbed. "Let's try going upstream, maybe there's an easier way."

She nodded and they followed the river's edge. He rejected a series of rocks that would involve jumping about three feet from one wet rock to another. "We'll come back if we have to."

After another couple of hundred yards he said, "Aha!" and pointed. A fallen tree made a sort of bridge across the river. He climbed up first, then reached for her hand and helped her up. The downed cedar was solid and wide, but branches and dampness meant they had to step carefully. He kept hold of her hand all the way across. Once they'd climbed down again, he grabbed her close and kissed her. Then, once more, they hiked west.

Today's hike wasn't a lot different than yesterday's except for the knowledge that she and the man hacking through bush ahead of her were now intimate.

Instead of imagining what he looked like naked, she knew. Her hands had caressed the lines of muscle in his back, she'd clutched at those shoulders that were bunching and flexing with the effort of widening their path.

They were together. Somehow, they'd make it.

THEY HIT THE logging road around two in the afternoon. Claire was so tired she was putting one foot in front of the other automatically and barely registered the change of terrain from narrow, root-and-rock-studded path to wide-open gravel until Max yelled, "We did it!"

She looked up and they were on an honest-to-goodness logging road.

A smile of relief bloomed on her lips. "We did it!" she yelled back at him. She forgot how tired she was as she ran over and threw herself at him. Laughing, they kissed and hugged and she knew they'd made it.

"I have no idea how long we'll have to walk to get to civil—" She stopped talking when she heard a sound so wonderful she thought she might be dreaming. It was the whine of a big engine working hard.

Within minutes, a logging truck appeared, trailing dust clouds. She had no idea if hikers ever came this way, but so there'd be no doubt that they were in need of help, she ran out into the road and waved crazily. The truck geared down, crested the hill and stopped on a flat stretch of road just ahead of them.

They ran to the cab window. Two sunburned guys in ball caps looked out at them.

"Do you have a phone?" Max asked.

"You the two that went missing in a small plane two days ago?"

She and Max exchanged glances. "Yep."

"Welcome back. There's a whole heap of people looking for you."

After that, it was less than half an hour before a chopper was landing on that flat stretch of gravel road.

They scrambled into the helicopter and she discovered she knew the pilot. His name was Steve and he worked for a helicopter company called Mountain Wing Adventures.

"How's Grandma?" Claire said as soon as she climbed on board.

"Lynette's fine, apart from worried about you, of course. Anybody hurt?"

"No."

"Good." And he handed them both bottles of water.

Even though Steve had reassured her about Lynette, she could not rest until the chopper landed and she saw that familiar and much-loved figure standing outside the office watching the landing. Lynette wasn't the only one, Claire realized. Almost a dozen pilots and mechanics stood with her. Pretty much the entire staff of Polar Air was here.

As soon as it was safe, she tumbled out of the chopper and ran for Lynette. She realized that the assembled staff were all cheering.

Her grandmother reached for her. They hugged and hugged. She felt a tremor running through Lynette and realized her grandmother was crying.

Tears were something she'd witnessed from her grandmother maybe three times in her life.

"It's okay. I'm safe. You're safe. We're fine." To her shock she realized her own cheeks were wet.

"I was so scared I was going to lose you," Lynette said when she could finally speak.

"You didn't."

"Are you all right?" Her grandmother ran her hands down Claire's arms as though checking for damage.

"I'm fine. Tired and sick of these clothes, but fine."

She turned to accept hugs and backslaps from the crew. Max was being welcomed home in the same fashion, though there were fewer hugs and more backslaps in his case.

She realized that he'd already become part of their team, more so now that he'd endured this ordeal with her and they'd both emerged unharmed. He'd gone from being the new guy, the one who still had to prove himself to gain acceptance, to a man who'd earned the respect of the crew at Polar Air.

He'd obviously cemented himself in Lynette's esteem, too, based on the huge hug he was receiving from her grandmother.

After the hugs and congrats, she noticed Tom Richter, a reporter from the local paper, was waiting to talk to her.

"Hi, Tom," she said.

"Glad to see you home safe," he said. Tom was in his late twenties. He'd come to Spruce Bay as an intern at the *Spruce Bay Sentinel* after getting a degree in journalism. Jobs were scarce in the field and Tom was clearly never going to be *New York Times* material. He'd stayed in town after his internship, made Spruce Bay his home. As tired as she was, understood he had a job to do.

"Thanks. Glad to be home."

"I'd like to do an interview with you and Max Varo when you get a minute."

"Sure. Of course. But give me a day, will you? I need to take a shower, eat some decent food that isn't fish and sleep in a real bed first."

"No problem. Can I get a picture now? For the front page of this week's paper?"

She understood that, like it or not, she was news, but she had her vanity. "I'm a mess. I don't want my photograph in the paper looking like I just spent three days in the bush."

"Okay. I got a few shots when you first got off the chopper." He looked at his camera with dislike and she suspected he wasn't too keen on the fact that he was a photojournalist whether he liked it or not. The *Spruce Bay Sentinel* couldn't afford a photography department. "I'm not sure how good they are."

"When you interview us tomorrow you can get a picture if you need one."

"Okay." He put away his camera. "I'll interview the chopper pilot. Get his take on the rescue."

"Good plan. I'm going to shower."

Tom's cell phone rang. He answered it and his voice sharpened. "What? Are you sure? He's dead?"

He shoved his phone away. "Gotta go. Man, what a week for news."

"What happened?" Lynette asked. "Who's dead?"

The reporter turned. "Frank Carmondy. Car accident. He wrapped his vehicle around a tree. Must have been headed on a trip. He had a bunch of stuff in the back and the first person on scene said the car smelled like a brewery. There was an open bottle of scotch on the seat beside the um—Frank."

Lynette wavered for a moment and both Max and Claire reached for her, but she held on. "Frank was on the phone regularly asking if there was any news of you. Honestly, he sounded as worried as I was. I know we've had our differences, but when you were in trouble he couldn't have been more concerned. When I told him they'd found you and were bringing you home, he was so happy he couldn't say anything for a full minute. He told me how glad he was that you were safe and his voice sounded so strange I think he might have been crying."

"You talked to him what? An hour ago?" Max asked.

Lynette nodded, sadness showing in her eyes. "About that."

Tom said, "Did he sound drunk?"

Lynette made a helpless gesture. "I was so happy I couldn't say."

"He must have left right away. His car was found fifty miles out of town, heading south. Wow. What a week for Polar Air. I better go, but I'll be back tomorrow."

"Thank God Frank was alone," Lynette said.

"What was he doing so far from town?"

"Such a tragedy," Lynette sighed.

Max and Claire exchanged glances. "Sounds like karma to me," Max muttered.

"Come on up to the house and let me get you something to eat," Lynette said. "I'll grieve for Frank tomorrow. Today, I will not have my happiness marred. My baby's back safe and sound." She kept patting Claire on the back as though she needed to feel that she was real and whole and truly unharmed.

"We need to see about retrieving the aircraft," Max said.

"You need to see about a nap, young man," Lynette told him, with a hands-on-her-hips stance that brooked no opposition.

"Okay. But I want back on the schedule tomorrow." He gave her a steely-eyed stare that wasn't a bad counterattack to the hands-on-hips thing. Claire watched with interest as two of the strongest wills she'd ever known butted up against each other.

"We'll see what the doctor says."

"No doctors," she and Max said in unison.

Lynette made a rude noise. "Neither of you are flying anywhere until you are cleared by a physician." She shook her finger at both of them. "And you know it."

Because they both did they muttered but quit arguing.

"Now, I've got hot soup on the stove and as much food as you can eat."

"Shower first," Claire said.

Max nodded. "Me, too. I need some clean clothes, as well." He grinned suddenly. "But I'll take you up on the food. Give me twenty minutes."

When she stepped inside Lynette's home the smell of coffee was more than she could resist. She went straight to the pot, poured herself a fresh mug, added milk and sugar, and closed her eyes to fully enjoy the first sip. "You don't know how good coffee tastes until you're deprived," she said.

"Take it with you."

She did, thankful that she still kept spare clothes at Lynette's place. She'd head back to her own small house on the property soon enough. For now she wanted to be fussed over.

When Claire returned to the kitchen feeling clean again and wearing a fresh shirt and a faded pair of jeans, Max was already there. Like her, he was sipping coffee.

He'd managed a remarkable transformation in a short time. The scruffy, unkempt man she'd been with for the past few days was once again the clean-cut, tidy Max Varo she'd first met. He was clean-shaven, wearing a crisp white shirt. She'd have assumed it was brand-new except that all his shirts appeared freshly ironed all day long.

His jeans held a suspicious crease that made her think he might have ironed them, as well.

Their gazes connected and she felt a slight shift occur, as though now that they had washed off the outer effects of their wilderness experience, some of their wild intimacy had washed off along with it. She felt his slight stiffness around her, a formality that they'd dispensed within the bush.

"Sit down," Lynette said. "I'm dishing up soup and I've got sandwiches and fruit coming up."

Max waited until Claire was seated before sitting beside her. As he settled their arms brushed and a rush of lust hit her. He shifted his chair farther away, probably afraid of burning his shirt from the heat they generated. She had to accept that they could try to put a little distance between them but their bodies weren't interested in playing along.

13

MAX HAD A problem. In fact, he had several of them. And when he spent any time at all thinking about them he realized that all his problems were related.

To Claire.

To the bravest, most amazing woman he'd ever known. When the plane had started to go down he'd seen her face, watched the fierce battle she'd fought. She hadn't panicked, not for a second. And she knew, likely better than he, how desperate their situation was. She'd kept her head and saved both their lives.

Was that the moment he'd realized he was in love with her?

Or was it later, when she'd cheerfully made the best of things on their hike out of the bush? With her plane underwater and her business in further peril.

Or was it later still when their bodies had joined and he'd felt something he'd never felt before in all his years of dating and enjoying women?

He couldn't pinpoint exactly when it had happened. All he knew was that he had fallen for the woman whose company he was planning to buy and return to profitability.

Which was great except for the small fact that he hadn't bothered to tell her why he was really working for Polar Air.

Had he become arrogant? Rich enough that he did whatever the hell he pleased without considering how his actions might affect others?

He'd gone to Spruce Bay on a lark, planning to find out what was going on at Polar Air without revealing his true reasons for being there. His undercover operation had never seemed underhanded to him, but when he looked at the situation through Claire's eyes he had a bad feeling she wouldn't agree. Especially now. She was still reeling from the knowledge that she'd been betrayed by one man who worked for her.

He didn't want to be the second.

Betrayal.

Disloyalty.

He didn't like the way either notion sat like lead in his gut.

The burning continued as he visited Doc Bouton, with his gray hair in a ponytail and toenails that needed cutting hanging over his well-worn Birkenstocks.

"You hit your head on the way down?" Doc demanded as he shone a light into Max's eyes.

"Nope."

"Hmm." He tested reflexes, asked a lot of questions. After twenty minutes he said, "You were damned lucky."

"I was damned lucky to have Claire Lundstrom in the pilot's seat."

Doc cracked a grin. "That's what I meant."

"So? Am I cleared for takeoff?"

"You really want to fly right away? After nearly getting killed out there?"

It was Max's turn to grin. "Hell, yeah."

But the grin faded when he returned to Polar Air to find Claire with an expression of worry on her face.

"Everything okay?"

She forced a smile. "It will be. It's not helping the bottom line that we're down a plane, and I've got a ton of paperwork to fill out. There's an insurance claim. And the plane's got to be salvaged and the cause of the crash investigated." The smile turned to a comical frown. "I hate paperwork."

"I know."

"Plus, the mine still wants that piece of equipment." She drummed her fingertips against the counter beside the computer. "I need to fly to Anchorage, get a replacement and deliver it up to them."

"You're planning to fly that route again?" He was a pretty hardy pilot but the thought of doing that very route again so soon made his stomach feel a little woozy.

"Gotta get back on the horse, Max."

He suspected that she was putting on a tough act. "Let me go," he said impulsively.

She shook her head. "I need to do this." Her gritted teeth confirmed his theory about the tough act. "We need to keep the mine's business and I need to get back in the air. It's like lightning striking twice. Doesn't happen."

"Statistically, that's not actually true. Lightning has no memory of where it's struck. It can and does strike the same place twice."

Her stare was wide and long. "Are you trying to scare me?"

"No. Sorry. Sometimes I let my geek side take over from my common sense. Tell me what you want me to do."

She nodded briskly. "I need you to pick up a pair of ice climbers. It's a prearranged pickup. Then you deliver them to Anchorage for their flight home."

His gaze never left her face. He didn't want her to fly up to the mine. It was stupid, he knew, but when you loved a woman, he discovered, logic wasn't always the strongest force. "How long will you be gone?"

"Couple of days. Don't worry. I'll be back in time for the funeral."

"Funeral?"

"Frank's."

"You know he tried to kill you."

She looked so sad he wished he hadn't mentioned it. "Innocent until proven guilty." She glanced out the window to where their small fleet of aircraft lived. "And whatever happened to him, he was part of our lives for a long time. I guess I want to say goodbye to the man he once was."

He was moving before he even realized it. He stepped close, pulled her to her feet and kissed her.

Her cheeks turned pink and he saw her glance around to make sure no one had seen the kiss. "What was that for?"

"Because I—"

He was interrupted by the door banging open. "Claire, I can't find black stockings. Do you have any?" It was Lynette and she sounded winded, like she'd been hurrying.

Max put an extra step's distance between him and Claire. He'd been about to blurt out that he loved her. Right in the operations center of an airline. What had happened to his legendary smoothness around women?

The woman he loved turned until her back was to him. "I don't think so. I can get you some in Anchorage."

"Oh, good. I haven't worn a dress in damn near twenty years, but I think Frank would like it." She looked at Max. "Glad you're cleared to fly. We need to show everyone, from our clients to our competitors, that it's business as usual."

"I'm off now to pick up some ice climbers."

"For God's sake don't crash the plane."

He paused on his way out. "Not planning on it."

HE RETRIEVED THE ice climbers without incident, then transported a new camp cook and fresh supplies out to a logging operation.

As he flew over craggy, glacial peaks reaching icy fingers toward him, he realized he was falling in love with this place. It had snuck up as quietly as his love for Claire. He tried not to worry about her. She knew what she was doing. Frank wasn't around to hurt her or her aircraft. He had to trust she'd be fine.

Still, after he'd cooked himself dinner, he was glad he'd planned an online visit with his buddies.

Max sat at the small desk in his small house and connected with Dylan and Adam. Both were lounging on Dylan's couch, beer in hand.

"You didn't make practice this week," Dylan complained. "In fact, you haven't made practice at all."

"I know. And I'm sorry about that. But things are crazy up here."

"She's just a girl," Adam said, and took a punch to the shoulder from Dylan.

"Shut up! If he's in luuuv, I win the bet." Dylan took a swig of beer. "You in luuuv, bro?"

The thing with Dylan and Adam, Max mused, was that there were no boundaries. At least, not between the three of them. Maybe they'd known each other too long. And with these two, he didn't even think about hedging. "Yes," he said. "I am."

At least he had the pleasure of watching Dylan choke on his beer and start coughing. Adam even lost his never-show-emotion cop face for a second as his eyes widened in surprise. "Seriously?" Adam asked, recovering first. "You're in love."

"Oh, yeah."

"But—but, you're a legendary commitment phobe. You date swimsuit models and women guys like Dyl and me could only dream about."

"Speak for yourself," Dylan said, recovering.

"Is it the hockey-playing bush pilot?" Adam couldn't have sounded more astonished.

"It is. And she is the most amazing woman I've ever met."

"Don't want to spoil your party, but don't forget you're in Alaska. Lot o' guys. Not many women. Maybe your judgment's skewed."

A picture of Claire flashed through his mind and he realized she'd have wowed him anywhere on earth. "She saved my life," he said.

Dylan straightened. "Well, that doesn't mean you have to marry her."

Adam ignored his friend. "What do you mean, she saved your life?"

As briefly as he could, Max told them both about Frank Carmondy, the crash, his suspicions. Carmondy's death. He didn't tell them that he and Claire had spent two nights in the bush, alone. Some things, he knew he'd never share.

"That's some serious stuff you got going on up there," Adam said. His eyes had narrowed and Max knew that meant he was considering the facts the way he would if this was one of his cases. "There will be an investigation, of course."

"Yeah. I think it will show that the plane was tampered with. That crash wasn't an accident. It was sabotage. I'm sure of it. And then the attention will turn to Carmondy."

"Are you sure it was him?"

"Oh, yeah. Nobody else would want to hurt Claire or the business. It had to be him."

"You want me to call a contact in Alaska? Find out what they know?"

Did he? He couldn't think of any benefit to finding out sooner when his gut told him the truth would come out at an inquiry.

"No. Let's let justice take its course. And, believe me, it will."

"But he's already dead. Why do you care so much?"

"Because I want Claire and Polar Air's reputations cleared. She's a hell of a pilot and the company's a good one."

"I guess you've considered that if the company's reputation is tarnished by the crash and whatever was going on, then you'll be able to get a better deal on buying the airline."

"I don't want a better deal. Damn it, I want to save the company. For Claire."

For long seconds no one spoke. Then Max asked the question that had been nagging at him all day. "Have I become arrogant?" He knew there weren't many people in the world who would give him an honest answer. These were two of them. Probably the only two. "I flew in thinking this would be fun. Relieve some of my boredom from spending too much time in the corporate world. I could fly a plane, get to know this company and see whether it was a turnaround candidate. See whether I wanted to buy it. I didn't think how my actions might affect the people here on the ground." He took a sip of soda water. "How they would affect Claire."

"Are you arrogant?" Adam repeated the initial question. "Sure. You can be. But if it was a problem you know we'd tell you. I don't know how you could be as successful as you are, as freakin' genius as you are, and not get arrogant sometimes. It must be tough to always be the smartest person in the room."

This wasn't the answer Max had hoped to hear.

Adam continued, "But maybe the real question you're trying to ask is, should you tell Claire who you really are? And I gotta tell you, in my opinion, the answer is yes."

Max stared out the window, saw the small fleet of planes that made up Polar Air. "You know, Adam, sometimes you are the smartest person in the room."

"And I'm the best-looking," Dylan said. "So what? You'd be crazy to tell her. Copping to why you're really there is a one-way ticket to the doghouse and you know it." He took another pull of beer. Then he suddenly sat forward and upright, like a wasp had stung him in the ass. "You know what this is like? Like that reality show, *Undercover Boss.*"

"Undercover Boss?" Max said, imagining he sounded as revolted as he felt.

"You watch reality shows?" Adam asked at the same time, sounding equally revolted.

"You should watch this show. Every episode follows a boss who goes undercover and goes on the factory floor or whatever, pretending to be a grunt, and gets his hands dirty with the working people. Then, at the end, when he's learned about their lives and their problems there's a big reveal. And maybe he gives the guy whose mom needs an operation a fat check to pay for it. Something like that."

Max really wished he didn't see the parallel.

"How do the employees react when they find out the big boss has been working with them undercover?"

"Sometimes it's great," Dylan said. "There's hugs and tears and everybody goes home happy." He glanced at Adam, then turned his face fully toward Max. "And sometimes they wind up and punch him in the face." He shrugged. "Any idea which way Claire's going to go?"

"Yeah," he said, rubbing his face. "I've got a pretty good idea."

14

CLAIRE FLEW THE replacement part up to the mine and then had to transport two mining executives to Anchorage on the return trip. She'd just said goodbye to the two suits when she received a text message. Her heart did a foolish little skip when she saw that it was from Max.

Her heart skipped even more foolishly when she read the text. Will you go on a date with me Thursday night?

A date. She hadn't had a date with a man who excited her as much as Max Varo in—well, she ruefully suspected it might be forever. She'd dated plenty of guys, spent too long with a couple of them and had grown extremely selective in the past couple of years.

You're cooking me dinner?

No. This is a going-out date.

Which made her wonder about wardrobe choices. Will I need a dress? she texted back.

Wear whatever you like. You always look good.

Hardly helpful, but then, in her experience, men

never understood the intricacies of choosing what to wear. She tried again:

Where are we going?

He texted back: Secret.

What time?

I'll pick you up at six.

Pick her up? They were living on the same property. Sometimes his obsessively good manners made her shake her head. Still, she liked the idea of going out on a date with Max. He'd surprised her in so many ways already, she wondered what Thursday night would bring. Passion, for sure, that was a given. She decided not to press him.

I'll be ready.

She could take off right now and be home in a couple of hours. Or...

She called the Spruce Bay Inn and asked for Laurel. Her friend sounded distracted when she answered.

"Busy day?"

"A bear got into the garbage. Terrified a couple of tourists. Made a mess everywhere. Timmy, the newest kitchen helper, didn't show up for work. Again. And I broke the heel off my favorite pair of shoes."

"Not the purple Ferragamos?"

"Yes!"

"Oh, no. Tragedy."

"But that's not why you're calling."

"No. I'm on a sleuthing mission. Did Max by any chance make a reservation for dinner on Thursday?"

"Hardly anyone makes reservations except on Fridays or Saturdays."

"Max would. Believe me. He's the kind of man who leaves nothing to chance."

"Sounds kind of dull."

She chuckled, thinking of the days they'd spent in the bush and all the ways he'd surprised her. "He's anything but."

"Okay. Hang on. I'll check."

Laurel was back in a couple of minutes. "No. No reservations for Max. Or Varo. In fact, there aren't any reservations at all for Thursday dinner. At least, not yet."

"Okay. Thanks."

"Oh, no, you don't. I've got trash-eating bears, freaked-out tourists, a major wardrobe malfunction and that bear was hibernating last time I had a date. You owe me. Details."

Claire felt the silly girlish rush of emotion as she said, "I seriously like him."

"You were trapped in the wilderness with this guy for days and you still like him?"

"Oh, yeah."

"I think my day just improved."

"But if he's not taking me to the Inn for our date, where's he taking me?"

"Why don't you ask him?"

"I did. He says it's a secret."

"Men! How are you supposed to know what to wear?"

"Exactly," she said, delighted that Laurel understood her predicament.

"Wear a dress."

"Why?"

"Because you have great legs and after spending days in the bush with the guy, he should see you in a dress."

When she thought back to how grubby she'd been during their hike to civilization, she had to agree with Laurel. "And if he's taking me to Micki's Pizzeria and Tavern?" Micki's was the only other place in town where you could sit down and eat.

"Then you'll be the one person in Micki's wearing a dress." She laughed. "He's not taking you to Micki's. He'll bring you here. I think we're getting some amazing scallops fresh in on Thursday. Just so you know."

"I am partial to scallops."

"Shall I reserve you one of my best rooms? Just in case?"

The thought of her and Max in a real hotel bed had her stomach clenching with sudden lust. But she didn't want to seem too eager. "No. I'll wing it."

SHE SPENT A couple of minutes trying to recall what was in her wardrobe and ended up calling Lynette and telling her she'd be a couple of hours later than planned. "I'm going shopping. I'll pick up your black stockings."

Then, shaking her head at her own foolishness, Claire grabbed a cab and went shopping.

She found herself feeling whimsical and romantic as she flipped through racks of dresses. Maybe the days in the bush and the near-death experience had affected her more than she'd realized, she thought. She was drawn to silks and soft colors, to a rack of lingerie as flimsy as it was expensive. The stuff was handmade, of silk and lace. She imagined Max's eyes on her as he undressed her, imagined his hands on her as he peeled off the wisps of fabric.

"This is very popular with brides," a saleswoman said, the slightest hint of a question in her tone.

She opened her mouth to say, "I'm not getting married," and instead found herself saying, "I can't decide between the ivory and the ice-blue."

The woman came closer. "With your coloring, and your beautiful eyes, I'd go with the ice-blue. It's gorgeous against your skin."

She would never normally have spent so much money on lingerie, she thought later. Maybe when you almost died, you worried less about paying bills and putting money aside for a rainy day. At this point, she was simply happy to know she was going to see some more rainy days.

And if she spent some of those rainy days inside, with Max, wearing the most expensive lingerie she'd ever owned, then that was fine with her.

The dress she chose was also blue and did indeed show off her legs.

Maybe her bank account was lighter, but so was her mood as she stashed her bags and headed up into the clouds toward home.

It was the time of year when days were long, nights were short and it was easy to forget that winter would soon be back demanding constant vigilance. Nights would seem to last forever, days would end in midafternoon and the snow and cold would be relentless. Many a Southerner had run screaming from an Alaskan winter, never to return. It was that first winter that showed a person what they were made of and if they could ever be at home in Alaska.

Would Max make it through his first winter? she wondered idly.

And did she want him to?

She not only liked and respected Polar Air's newest pilot, but to her surprise she'd discovered that under those pressed white shirts and ironed jeans was a man who finally made her understand what the term *Latin lover* could really mean.

Hot, hot sex, as inventive as it was raw. He was a man of contrasts, Max. A true gentleman, polite and reserved, but to her amazement and delight, he left all his reserved politeness at the bedroom door.

Or in their case, outside the confines of the forest.

She suspected he'd be exactly as wild and certainly more inventive when he had all the comforts of civilization. It wasn't that he stopped being a gentleman in bed. He was giving and generous, making sure her pleasure came before his own. Sometimes, she recalled with a tilting of her lips, making sure her pleasure came again and again before his own. She wondered if they'd wait for their date on Thursday before getting naked again, and realized she hoped it wouldn't be that long.

She banked, radioed her route to Lynette and wondered again if Max would make it through a winter.

Her credit card balance mocked her. The bags in the back of the plane mocked her. A woman who purchased pricey lingerie for a man was not planning a short-term fling.

She really hoped his South American blood could figure out how to handle a winter in Alaska.

But today the sun was shining and she had a date she was looking forward to. For now, that was enough.

15

WHEN CLAIRE RAN into the Spruce Bay Inn Thursday after she knew the lunch crowd would be gone, she sought out Laurel in her office. When she walked in, she found her friend staring at her computer screen with an expression of loathing on her face. "Bears get into the trash again?"

Her friend gave a crow of delight, jumped out of her chair and hugged Claire.

"I haven't seen you since you came back from the dead. How are you?"

"Good enough that I went shopping."

Laurel put a perfectly manicured hand to her chest. "You took my advice. Did you get a dress?"

"And underwear. And shoes."

"Oh, be still my heart." She spied the bags Claire had brought in. "Let me see."

Claire first gestured to the computer screen. "Looked like you were dealing with something nasty. Do you want me to wait?"

"Oh, no. Just the wheat-belly diet." She made a face. "Have you seen that thing?" She shook her head. "I cannot live without bread."

"Nor should you."

"Gimme," she said, grabbing at a bag.

When she saw the dress, she nodded enthusiastically. "Perfect. It's feminine, classic, will accentuate the hell out of your figure."

Claire pulled out the lingerie and watched her friend's eyes bug out of her head. She held the barely-there bra over her chest and said, "What do you think?"

"Oh, oh. I'm not even gay and I want to have sex with you. Max will be lost." They both spent a quiet moment in lust with the lingerie. Then Laurel said, "Okay. Shoes. Must. See. The. Shoes."

Since both women agreed that you have to see shoes on to appreciate them, Claire pulled off her leather boots and socks and lifted the lid of the shoe box. Inside were nestled a pair of Stuart Weitzmans that looked like they had been created to go with that dress. And that underwear.

They were strappy, silvery blue, and had heels that were high but not nosebleed high. Claire thought she might actually be able to walk in them. At least fifty feet or so.

"No!" Laurel cried when Claire pulled up her jean legs to show off the shoes.

"No?" Some of her pleasure leaked out. She loved those shoes, had been sure Laurel would, too.

"Oh, the shoes are great. But you cannot insult Stuart by putting his gorgeous sandals on those feet." She shook her head. "Pedicure. Now."

"But Max is coming at six. I have paperwork."

"This is an emergency. You can do your paperwork tomorrow. Believe me, it will wait." She grabbed one of Claire's hands and said, "These nails can't. Good thing I hire and fire the spa people here. I bet they can fit you in."

While Laurel called down to the hotel spa, Claire checked out her feet. They had gripped the rudder and fought strong currents and a broken elevator, they had hiked miles and miles through bush. She'd clipped her toenails when she'd returned home, so they were straight and utilitarian. And colorless. Her feet were callused and the skin rough. How had she forgotten, in all her preparations, to pretty up her hardworking feet?

"You can go right on down," Laurel said. "They'll take care of you. Ask for Ginny."

"Thanks."

"Oh, and it's my treat."

When Claire protested, her friend said, "Hey, I'm just glad to see you back safe and sound. We were worried about you."

"It's good to be home."

"I've told the waitstaff to reserve the best table for you. You know, the one in the alcove with the view." Claire knew that tourists and locals alike fought over that table. She was genuinely touched.

"So, Max did reserve."

"No, but where else are you going to eat in Spruce Bay?"

"I owe you big-time," she said, hugging her friend.

"And you'll pay me back," Laurel said. "With details. Lots and lots of delicious details."

CLAIRE NOT ONLY consented to the pedicure and manicure, but she let the stylist talk her into a makeup application. She drew the line at the hair, preferring her own simple style.

She felt a little foolish putting so much effort into a

date with a man who hadn't even bothered to book a table, but then, as Laurel had reminded her, she wasn't primping for Max. She was doing it for herself. And so as not to insult those shoes.

When she opened the door to Max who arrived promptly at six, she had the pleasure of seeing his eyes warm with approval when he looked at her.

"You are so beautiful," he said, stepping forward to give her lips a light kiss that didn't muss her carefully applied makeup, but promised so much more for later. Okay, so she hadn't done the primping for Max. Didn't mean she wouldn't enjoy the effect the stylist's efforts had on him.

Max had also gone to some effort. She thought his hair bore the signs of a recent trim, he was freshly shaven and wore a sports jacket with gray slacks. The clothes fit him beautifully, almost as though they'd been handmade for his frame.

"I wasn't sure what to wear," she said.

"You look perfect. Ready?" On her nod, he took her hand and led her outside. When she headed toward his truck—the only shiny one in the parking area—he urged her in the other direction.

"Where are we going?"

"I told you, it's a surprise." In seconds she realized they weren't going to be traveling by car at all. Seemed they were flying. In Max's plane.

"I assumed we were eating in town," she said as he helped her into the plane.

"You must eat there all the time," he said. "I wanted to take you somewhere special."

No wonder he hadn't bothered making a reservation at the Spruce Bay Inn. If they were going somewhere more special than the dining room at the inn, she was happier than ever that she'd succumbed to the instinct to shop.

She waited until he'd done his checks and Lynette had cleared him for takeoff and wished them a good evening.

"Lynette was in on this?"

"Of course. I needed her cooperation since I don't plan to have us back until midmorning tomorrow."

"Tomorrow, but I have—"

"You don't have anything until the afternoon. I checked. And neither do I. Lynette will take care of anything that comes up." When she opened her mouth to speak, he stopped her, saying, "Lynette said you'd argue. She told me to remind you that she ran this airline just fine for more years than you've been alive."

She closed her mouth again and decided to simply enjoy the fact that Max had gone to so much trouble to plan a rather long date.

"I don't even have a toothbrush."

"Yes, you do."

"Nightdress?"

He sent her a look. "Do you think you'll need one?"

As their gazes connected, hot shivers danced along her skin. She moistened her lips with her tongue and felt heat pulling her and Max closer. "No," she said and found her throat had gone dry, her voice husky. "No, I don't believe I will."

They were climbing up into the sky, and she took a moment to enjoy the coastline from the copilot seat, something she rarely did anymore. Sun sparkled off waves that splashed playfully against the shores, making it difficult to remember that those same seas crashed with menace against the frozen shoreline most of the year.

"Are you ever going to tell me where we're going?"

"I'm going to let you decide."

"What?"

He smiled at her tone. His hands were light and confident on the controls; he handled that plane with such assurance and deftness it reminded her of the way he'd handled her. "You have a choice. I've booked a popular restaurant in Anchorage that includes a dance floor. It's been written up in Zagat." He mentioned the name of the place and her eyes widened. She'd heard of it. It was amazingly popular, trendy and very expensive. She'd never been and couldn't imagine how he'd managed to snag a reservation at such short notice, never mind how he could afford to eat there.

Then she recalled her own lavish spending on clothes and assumed that Max, too, was feeling the need to celebrate being alive. Maybe they were both going a little overboard but they'd rein it in soon enough, she was sure.

"What's the other choice?"

"A little bed-and-breakfast in a somewhat remote location. The chef came from a Michelin-starred restaurant in Paris, fell in love with the scenery here and opened his own place. It has a reputation of being quiet and intimate. It's possible we'll be the only guests." Visions of the two of them alone at the wilderness B and B quickly moved into X-rated territory. She stirred, crossed her legs.

Two very different choices. A splashy night out with a lot of people in a happening restaurant or an intimate dinner followed by an intimate night. In fairness, she assumed the restaurant meal in Anchorage would also end with a night in a hotel. "Which one do you prefer?" she asked him.

He shook his head. "Lady's choice."

"You've booked both?"

"Yes. I'll cancel whichever one you don't choose."

"The B and B."

When he glanced over at her and smiled, she suspected he'd have made the same choice.

THEY LANDED WITH only the slightest of bumps. She doubted she could have landed more smoothly. The guy really knew his stuff. She unbelted and pushed open her door and before Max could jump down, another man was waiting to help her to the ground. When she thought about how often she was the one helping passengers alight and then hauling their heavy packs and equipment out for them, she decided it was kind of fun to be treated as though she were made of glass for a change.

As she stepped down onto the grass, her freshly manicured nails caught the light and seemed to wink at her. "Welcome," the man said. "I hope you had a good trip. I am your host, Felix."

He was adorable with his black hair and his French accent. He didn't say *hope,* he said *'ope* and *host* was *'ost.* He wore jeans and a navy shirt, a white apron wrapped about his waist as though he'd forgotten it was there.

"I will show you to your room to freshen up."

There were no signs of cars or other aircraft. She glanced at the B and B. It was small, but there was nothing rustic or shabby about it. Made from cedar and glass with an enormous porch out front that looked out on the river, she felt she could settle in here for a while. Raised garden beds burst with herbs and vegetables that she suspected she'd soon be tasting. Several Adirondack chairs painted a deep cranberry color and covered in soft cushions begged her to lounge outside with a cup of coffee and a book.

"What a beautiful spot," she said.

"Thank you. I enjoy it."

"Are we the only guests?"

He glanced at Max with brows lifted, then said to her, "But of course. Come."

He led them inside and up a wide-plank staircase. Native art covered the walls. When they reached the top of the stairs he led them to the left and through a large doorway. She cried out with delight when she saw the room. One wall was all window, overlooking the river, with a soaker tub in front of it. The opposite wall seemed to be all bed. The king-size bed also took advantage of the view. The decor was both simple and sumptuous and the bathroom was a sanctuary.

"This is amazing," she said.

"Thank you. I like to make your stay memorable. I will serve cocktails on the veranda whenever you are ready. Dinner at eight?"

At her nod, Max said, "That's fine. Thank you."

When Felix had gone, she threw herself at Max. "Oh, wow. I had no idea a place like this existed. How did you find it?"

He shrugged. "Friends recommended it."

"If the food is as good as this room, I am never leaving."

He chuckled. "The food's supposed to be excellent." He stroked a finger down her shoulder, followed the path with his lips. "And with what I have planned for later, you'll need the sustenance."

16

MAX CURSED HIMSELF for a fool. He should have told his assistant to be sure and swear Felix to secrecy. In fact, the secluded B and B had already had two bookings for tonight. The two parties had been more than happy to switch their reservations to another night when they'd found out that their stay would be paid for and a bottle of champagne thrown in as a thank-you. However, he didn't want Claire to know. Not yet.

He rarely traded on his absurd wealth by acting like a big shot, but tonight was his first real date with a woman he was already in love with. He had wanted everything to be perfect. And so far, he thought, enjoying Claire's bright, spontaneous happiness, it was.

He took her hand. Kissed it and held on as they walked downstairs and out to the veranda for cocktails. Felix had classical music playing. One of the Brandenburg Concertos spilled out as they settled into Adirondacks and sipped champagne cocktails.

When they went in for dinner the table was set with fine linens and fresh flowers. Every dish was locally sourced, from the nettle soup to the duck that their host raised himself to the cake made from eggs that Felix collected each day from his henhouse. Felix had pre-selected wines to go with each course so there was nothing for Max to do but enjoy his dinner companion.

He already knew she was an excellent pilot, a competent manager and a woman who could trek through the wilderness with toughness and good humor. He hadn't known, though he'd suspected, that she was a charming dinner companion.

They didn't talk about work. They avoided any mention of their recent ordeal by unspoken agreement. Instead, they spoke of music, and books they'd read. Of trips they had enjoyed or longed to take.

"I've always wanted to fly around the world solo," Claire said. The candlelight shone against her hair and made the wine in her glass sparkle. "I read a biography of Amelia Earhart when I was at school and decided I wanted to do that one day."

"Will you?"

She shrugged. "Who knows? It's bucket-list stuff. Some of those things are probably meant to remain dreams. But I haven't put it out of my mind. How about you?"

"Mars," he said.

"Mars?" She lowered her glass to stare at him. "The planet?"

"Sure. I want to go there. To set foot on it. Why not? They're already selling tickets for space tourism. It's only a question of time."

"And money," she reminded him. "Do you have any idea how much a ticket would cost to fly to space?"

He knew exactly how much since he'd already booked a spot on the first Virgin Galactic flight. When he chose not to reveal that fact to Claire, he experienced that mild burning discomfort once more. He wasn't lying, he told himself, when he withheld the truth about his wealth. He was simply choosing to keep some things to himself.

Max had never worried too much about revealing himself to women before. He found it was always a better policy to reveal too little than too much.

But Max had never been in love before, and as he sat here with Claire he discovered he wanted to tell her, not only about the flight he'd already booked, but about everything. He wanted her to understand how a series of childhood ear infections had destroyed his chances of following his dream. He wanted her to know all his likes and dislikes, his foibles and weaknesses, his history, his family, his friends.

He wanted her to be part of his life.

But he didn't tell her everything. On some level he understood that what stopped him was fear. He was afraid that if she knew exactly who he was and why he was here, she'd reject him.

He needed more time, time for her to get to know him better, to trust him completely. Then he could tell her all the things he wanted to tell her now.

So, instead of explaining that he'd already booked a seat and would make sure she was on the same flight with him if she wanted to go, he lifted his hands and said, "Like you said, it's bucket-list stuff."

Soon, he promised himself. Soon he'd tell her everything. Maybe wining and dining her, bringing her to this most exclusive of small inns, made him nothing but a crass billionaire trying to impress a woman with his wealth. But he was willing to use anything he could to win her.

When Felix put their dessert in front of them, some wonderful concoction of cake and raspberries—grown locally, of course—with a sauce that was pure magic and had Claire moaning with pleasure, he popped the cork on a bottle of vintage Cristal. The champagne bubbled into tall flutes. "Enjoy your dessert," Felix said, with a slight bow, preparing to depart.

"Thank you."

"This dessert is amazing," Claire said after Felix had disappeared.

"I can't even taste it," Max said, and amazingly it was true. "I can only think about tasting you."

Their gazes collided and he felt once more that rush of connection that was unique with Claire. When he gazed at her he felt as though she were seeing right down inside of him and he was seeing right down inside of her. As ridiculous as it was miraculous.

She pushed aside the remains of her dessert with a hand that trembled slightly. "Let's go to bed," she said.

He didn't need prompting. He rose, pulled the bottle of champagne from the bucket on the sideboard where it sat cooling, grabbed their glasses in his other hand and followed his woman.

When they got upstairs, she said, "I feel kind of nervous. Almost like it's our first time."

"It's not nerves," he said. "It's anticipation. It's knowing that we already give each other pleasure, but we're only beginning to learn all of each other's secrets, to share all of ourselves."

"Yes, that's exactly it. How did you understand so well?"

He gazed at her, her lips ready for his, her body, he instinctively knew, already aroused, her eyes both serious and sultry and he said, "I know because I feel exactly the same way." And then he leaned in and kissed her.

She tasted of the sweetness of raspberry, the sizzle of champagne, and of woman hot and ripe and ready.

He placed the champagne and the glasses on the bedside table. At some point, Felix or perhaps a hidden helper had turned down the bed. Two tiny wrapped chocolates lay on the pillows.

He tossed them aside, and turned to undress Claire. She stood as though suddenly shy and he understood he must take his time with her, treat her as reverently as she deserved. He kissed her again, began running his hands down her back, down her arms, until he felt her desire begin to build. He slipped the straps of her dress off her shoulders and began to kiss and nibble. The slide of the zipper revealed the long line of her back.

When the dress slid he stopped it, instinctively neat, and let her step out of it before laying the dress tidily over a chair back. Then he turned back.

And nearly lost it right there.

Claire, naked in the bush after a plane crash, was a gorgeous sight. Claire, with painted toes and shining hair, naked but for a couple of whispers of silk, was quite literally a breathtaking sight. Her luscious curves teased him through gossamer, her lips tilted in a way that compelled him to move closer. "You are more gorgeous than I remember."

"I'm not covered in dirt and leaves, that's why," she said softly, then pulled him closer so she could take her turn stripping him. He helped, too eager to linger, unbuttoning his shirt with impatience, yanking it over his head while she worked his belt, buttons and zipper. His pants fell to the floor and she reached for the throbbing bulge between his legs, caressing him through his cotton briefs, before slipping her hands into the waistband and sliding them down his hips. He kicked them away, tumbled her back onto the bed.

"As much as I love this lingerie," he told her, "it's going to have to come off."

"My shoes—"

"Leave them."

She shook her head at him, but lifted her shoulders, then her hips, so he could peel the barely-there underwear off her.

He had a whole night and the comfort of a big bed and he intended to use every minute, every inch, giving her an experience she would never forget.

He knew that he would never forget either. The look in her eyes, the smell of her skin, the feel of her lips against his, the taste of her.

He felt an urgent need to be inside her, but first he took the time to prepare her, stroking her with his fingers until she was wet and ripe, until her eyes had gone soft and misty and he felt the laxness in her muscles. She was beginning to toss and tiny sounds came out of her mouth, somewhere between a murmur and a gasp. Already he knew the signs that she was close.

He parted her thighs, raised himself over her and held her gaze with his as he slowly entered her. Her hips rose to meet him and she pulled him into her body, sucking him deep. She was already so close, and he found he was racing to catch up. She went wild beneath him, bucking against him, and when she grabbed his ass and dragged him hard into her he couldn't stop himself. He exploded even though he'd intended to wait until she'd crested, but even as he felt waves of bliss pound through him he heard her cries, felt her body spasm around him and knew that the bliss was shared.

He kept moving, slowing things down, enjoying the aftershocks, unwilling to break the intimate connection. She stroked his face and the simple gesture was as intimate as anything else they'd shared.

She said, "This is the first time we've had sex in a bed."

He looked deep into her eyes, as changeable as the endless sky during an Alaskan summer and said, "We're not having sex."

"We're not?" She wiggled her hips as though checking that their bodies were still connected.

He grasped both her hands in his, entwining their fingers. He began to move again, slowly, enjoying the exquisite feel of her soft, wet heat. "We're making love."

17

"I GUESS I'LL be making the flight of shame in last night's clothes," Claire said the next morning. It was worth it, she decided. It had been a night to remember. Her body ached deliciously. She stretched, as languid as a tabby cat in the sun.

Her companion, who could indulge in a marathon night of sex and still not have mussed hair, shook his head. "You won't. I planned ahead."

She hit him with a pillow. "Of course you did."

He chuckled and rolled on top of her, taking her wrists lightly in his hands and pulling them up and over her head. "Your grandmother packed a few things for you to choose from."

He kissed her mouth, and her chin, then began working his way toward her earlobe.

"She must approve of you to send me off like this and even pack me clothes for the morning."

"Of course she does. Grandmothers always approve of me," he said with a touch of arrogance.

"And why would that be? Because you charm them to get into their granddaughters' pants?"

He could put on a haughty look when he felt like it.

She'd noticed it a couple of times. For some reason she found it kind of endearing. "It's because they instinctively know I'm a gentleman."

She snorted. "There was nothing gentlemanly about you last night."

"You complaining?"

She pushed her body against him and nuzzled his neck where a little stubble reminded her he hadn't shaved. "Not hardly."

"Good." And then he began to make love to her all over again. She'd have thought she couldn't take any more, but to her amazement her response was fast and intense. He sent her over the edge twice before finally taking his pleasure. After a final, lingering kiss, he said, "Let's shower and get breakfast."

"I'm so sorry we didn't get time to enjoy that bathtub."

His gorgeous dark eyes gleamed. "Next time."

He must be banking on a lot of overtime if he thought he could afford this place again, she thought, but she merely nodded and headed to the shower with him. At least they could share that.

"I don't think I can eat after all that food last night," she said as she was toweling off.

"Okay. You have coffee. I will eat."

But, of course, her appetite returned with a vengeance when they got to the dining room and she not only smelled fresh coffee but was greeted with home-made muffins and fruit and offered a choice of waffles with various toppings, eggs Benedict with Felix's home-made hollandaise sauce or fresh muesli.

"You can choose one or all of the choices," Felix assured her, pouring fresh-squeezed orange juice into crystal glasses.

"I can't resist eggs Benny," she said.

Max ordered the same thing and added the muesli as well for good measure.

By the time they set off home, she felt as though she'd been away for a week. She had been thoroughly pampered, well fed and well sexed. No, she reminded herself, thinking of that wonderful moment last night. Well loved.

She glanced over at Max, hard to read behind his sunglasses, as he piloted the aircraft above the ragged lawn of trees.

Was it possible? Did he love her?

They'd only known each other a few weeks. But they'd been intense weeks. They'd worked together, practiced in the rink together, crashed and fought their way through the wilderness together. They'd made love.

No question their physical connection was deep and magical. But was it love?

She felt that she could fall, she may already have been teetering dangerously on the brink, but something stopped her from going all in.

Max was charming, he was generous, he was brave and the most amazing lover she'd ever known. But he was also reserved. She'd had the sense a few times that he was holding something back.

Not surprising, she supposed. A small town in Alaska like Spruce Bay drew all kinds of wanderers, adventurers, escape artists and ex-cons. People who couldn't, or wouldn't, make it in the lower 48. She'd put Max in the adventurer/wanderer category. Now she wasn't so sure. Was he escaping from something?

The trouble with a man who was on the move, whether for fun or due to fear, was that they tended to keep moving.

"You're thinking deep thoughts," Max said, giving her the disconcerting impression he'd read her mind.

"Not really." Then she decided to be honest. At least partly. "I'm wondering how you'll like Spruce Bay once winter comes. Whether you'll stay."

The little plane hit a patch of turbulence and he took a minute to steady them through it before answering, but she'd already seen the moment he went suddenly rigid.

When he turned to her, she wished he wasn't wearing the sunglasses. She wanted to see his eyes. He said, "I think I could be happy here."

She let it go, but it wasn't exactly an answer.

CLAIRE COULDN'T concentrate. When she stared at her computer screen, all she could see was a vision of Max and her at that amazing wilderness B and B. She couldn't figure out what was troubling her until she realized that Max hadn't seemed a bit overwhelmed by the sheer luxury of the place. She'd snuck a peek at the price list in the brochure she'd found in the bedside table and her eyeballs had practically popped out of her head. Then they'd had all those different wines and champagne that had a year on the label. She knew Cristal was a top brand and she might not be a wine connoisseur but she knew that if there was a date on the label it meant vintage, which meant even more pricey.

She also knew Max's salary.

And yet, when they'd gone to check out from the B and B and she'd discreetly tried to offer him her credit card to split the bill, he'd kissed her and told her it was his treat.

Which was nice. Generous. Fantastic.

But where the hell was Max Varo getting that kind of money?

And if he had it, why was he working for Polar Air?

She liked her theory about near-death experiences

leading to one-off spending sprees, but her extravagance had been limited to a few hundred dollars. He'd probably dropped a couple of grand to take her to the fancy lodge.

Okay, it wasn't enough money to break a man, he'd make that in a busy week, but maybe it was the way he acted, as though he lived like that all the time, that had thrown her.

It was like a sign when she got a text from Laurel that said, Where were u last night? Not here. Need deets.

Talking her confused feelings over with her friend was exactly what she needed. Laurel would talk her out of her foolishness. She immediately texted back: Need girl talk. You free later?

They decided to meet for a glass of wine at Laurel's place when they both got off work.

Laurel lived in a little house in town. She'd been given the option of living at the hotel when she'd first been offered the job but had firmly turned it down. She'd told Claire that in a small town where everybody gossiped, the last thing she needed was to live in the only decent hotel in town. It was gossip central. So, she'd bought a tiny, solid house that she'd turned into a charming escape. It was as feminine as an issue of *Victoria* magazine.

When Claire pulled up, having ridden her bike over for the exercise, she had to smile. Sunflowers, delphiniums and other colorful flowers she couldn't identify made the tiny front yard more like a painting than a garden. She left her bike by the front door and knocked then entered.

"Hiya," said Laurel, emerging from the kitchen trailed by heavenly cooking smells.

"Are you baking?"

"I begged an unbaked quiche off the chef and I'm throwing together a salad."

With a flourish, Claire pulled a box of chocolates from under her sweater. "And I brought dessert."

"No wonder we're best friends. Come on in. I thought we'd sit out back and enjoy the sunshine."

She loved Laurel's house. The living room was painted in a soft lavender color and furnished with chintz sofas and far too many cushions. A painting of Victorian ladies drinking tea dominated one wall. Her kitchen was as yellow as the sunflowers outside and a collection of bright pottery jugs lined the windowsill. A female soloist sang out from the iPod dock. Claire thought it might be Fiona Apple, but she wasn't certain.

"Whenever I come here, I think I should do something with my place," she sighed.

"Your place is fine. It suits you."

It was true, of course. The simple, clutter-free space was a snap to clean and everything in it was useful. "But I want this to suit me. I wish I was a girlie girl."

"And I wish I could fly a plane." Laurel tested her salad dressing, added more walnut oil. "And that I was thin." She began to drizzle salad dressing over her salad. "But it's probably never going to happen. I'm scared of heights and love food way too much."

Claire smiled. "Maybe we should both be happy with who we are."

"Good plan. Get the wine."

She opened the fridge, marveled at the number of items in it, took out a chilled bottle of white, blessed the invention of the screw-top wine bottle and retrieved stemware from the glass-fronted cabinet Laurel had picked up at a flea market.

Outside the kitchen door was a small patio with a metal table and chairs that looked as though they'd come from a café in Paris. Knowing Laurel, they probably had.

A jug of sweet peas sat on the table, which was already set with pretty place mats and cutlery.

"Okay," Laurel said, sitting down and taking a sip of her wine. "Tell me everything."

And so she did. She told Laurel about the surprise plane trip and the tiny B and B. And when she began to describe the place, Laurel said, "Wait a minute, I've heard of this place. The chef is famous, right?"

"He came from Paris. His name is Felix."

Laurel nodded crazily. "Felix Gerard. He's like famous. Story is, he wanted to get away from the snobbery of the Paris food scene. He wanted to provide an amazing, high-end experience in a remote location. He'd source locally as much as possible. I personally think he must have had a breakdown, but he found some venture capitalists to back him and the inn is like some hidden treasure. I heard you have to book months in advance to get in."

Claire wrinkled her brow. "Maybe he's not doing so well anymore. We were the only people there."

"But *Luxury Food and Travel Magazine* just did a feature on him. Like two months ago. You were so lucky to get in."

That strange feeling of discomfort came over her again.

"Tell me about the food."

Food? "But I'm having relationship issues."

"I know that, and I'm going to be the most supportive friend ever, but please, tell me about the food first."

So she did. Laurel moaned like a woman in the throes of the best sex of her life. "Those mushrooms. He grows them himself. I hope to go there one day before I die, and you get whisked off at a moment's notice." She shook her head. "Okay, tell me the rest. Was there sex? I need to know about the sex."

"It was great."

"Okay. In relation to the food? And we know that Felix Gerard's food is a ten."

"Then the sex was a twenty." Her body tingled at the mere thought of the sex. "Maybe twenty-five."

Laurel stared at her. "I'm going to need more wine."

And then they laughed, and she started to relax. As they enjoyed their dinner Claire realized how lucky she was that Laurel had moved to Spruce Bay to take the job as innkeeper.

They dug into the quiche and salad and the bread steaming in the basket—also courtesy of the inn kitchen—then Laurel said, "So, the place was amazing, the sex legendary. I don't think you're here for bragging rights. What's with the deer-in-the-headlights look?"

And that, Claire thought, was why they were best friends. Not only because they were two single women of approximately the same age with similar sensibilities, but because they got each other. She sighed. "I don't know. Everything's great except I'm getting this funny feeling that he's keeping something from me."

"You think he's married?"

"No!" The thought hadn't crossed her mind. She thought about it for a second. "No. It's not that. It's more that he's not entirely open."

"Sweetie, if you peeled open all of us who live here you'd find plenty of secrets. Look at me. I didn't move here for the climate."

"I know."

Even though they both knew the story, Laurel told it again. "I was living in Atlanta, running a boutique hotel. Part of a chain. They were grooming me for bigger things. Then I fell in love." She shook her head. "Never fall in love with a chef. Fickle artistes who think they're God's gift to food, never mind to women." She picked up a stem of arugula off her plate and nibbled absently. "He wooed me through food. He absolutely wooed me with food."

"I know."

"And then he dumped me for a waitress. A size-two Jersey girl with bigger boobs than brains."

"I know," she said soothingly.

"I may have said a few things to him that I shouldn't have, but I was so angry, so hurt."

"I know."

"And when he told management it was him or me—" she glanced at Claire as though she were pulling herself back into the present with an effort "—they chose him!"

"I know."

"So, when I looked for jobs I went for the ones that were the farthest geographically from Atlanta." She put the nibbled leaf back on her plate. "And Spruce Bay won hands down."

"Do you regret coming here?"

"First winter, I thought I'd die. I had that SAD syndrome people talk about. Not enough sun. And the relentless cold and snow was killing me. I figured I'd be out as soon as I could find another job. But somehow, this place got under my skin. I met people, including you. I run the hotel. And sure, I'm not being groomed as an executive in a chain of properties, but I like it here. I can't imagine moving."

"I know. It's that first winter that decides whether you'll stay or go."

Laurel shifted in her seat. "Wow, I sure made that all about me! I guess my point was that we all came here for a reason. It's not exactly on the beaten path, you know? I'm here because of heartbreak and corporate backstabbing, you're here because of a family tragedy. Max probably has reasons he'd rather not share with you. So long as he's not running from the law or something, does it really matter?"

"But why doesn't he tell me? We're intimate. We're sleeping together. He knows how I ended up here because I told him. We nearly died in a plane crash. We hiked out together, survived in the wilderness together. What is it that he can't tell me?"

"Didn't you do a background check when you hired him?"

"We're not exactly the CIA. We checked references, of course, his flying qualifications. His flying hours. He doesn't have a lot of Alaska hours but he's got thousands of Pacific Northwest hours which is close enough."

Laurel stacked plates and rose. "Did you do a Google search on him?"

"Do a Google search on him? No. He's a pilot, not a celebrity."

"You'd be surprised what a search engine can turn up. Look for him on Facebook? Twitter?"

She shook her head. "He's not on LinkedIn," she said, pleased she could at least offer that. She only knew because Lynette had asked him.

She rose, gathered the rest of the dishes and carried them into the kitchen. Laurel was loading the dishwasher.

Laurel said, "Take the rest of the wine and the glasses into my office. We'll see what turns up on the computer." She shot Claire a glance. "If you really want to know."

18

Did she want to know? Did she want a search engine to uncover whatever secrets it held about Max? She hesitated for a moment, then decided. Of course she did. Maybe if she'd been less trusting of Frank Carmondy she wouldn't have ended up swimming to shore across a freezing-cold lake while the plane she'd been piloting sank like a rock to the bottom.

"Yes," she said. "I'm in."

"We may not find anything," Laurel warned, "but it's worth a shot. I'm pretty good with a computer. I dated a techie guy when I did my business degree. He taught me a few things."

In a couple of minutes, Laurel had brought the chair from her dressing table into her home office and placed it beside her ergonomic office chair. The pair sat side by side while Laurel typed some letters into a search engine.

Claire waited, feeling an odd weightlessness in her belly. She wanted to know what the internet could reveal about Max Varo. She didn't want to know.

It wasn't too late to stop Laurel. To tell her to keep her typing fingers to herself. But she didn't. There was probably nothing there. And if there was, she wanted to know.

"You see? What did I tell you? Everybody's searchable," Laurel said with triumph.

She leaned forward, half eager, half dreading. And blinked. It wasn't Max Varo she was looking at on the screen. It was herself. "Where the hell did that come from?" she cried. The picture was taken at a Fourth of July picnic and fireworks display at a local park. In the photo, she was stuffing her face with potato salad. She'd imagined that if anyone had ever bothered to look for her on the internet they'd have discovered her picture on the official website of Polar Air. Not that some horrible snap of her stuffing her face would pop up. Even worse, there was a caption. *Local bush pilot Claire Lundstrom fuels up for her next flight.*

What if Max did the same sleuthing she and Laurel were doing? Was that the impression she wanted him to have of her?

"Must be from the local paper. I guess they uploaded a bunch of candids."

Claire groaned. "Make it go away."

With a few clicks, Laurel did. Then she typed Max Varo's name into the search engine.

"Hmm. Not much. And most of that is Spanish. Oh, wait, here's a Max Varo with a Facebook page." But when she clicked on it, the site obviously belonged to a teenager.

She kept clicking. "Here's a Maxwell Varon. Could he have shortened his name?" she mused. "Oh, no. Wait. This guy's a soccer player." They checked out the photo of a twentysomething in soccer shorts and a jersey who was blond and much younger than her Max. "Cute, though."

But not her Max. She began to feel better.

"It's weird not to find him at all. Do you think he's using an alias? Maybe he's wanted and he's hiding out in Alaska under an assumed name."

"Then how did he provide the references? They were from legitimate sources."

"Okay. Just trying to be helpful. Oh, look. Here's a Maximilian Varo. Hah, maybe he's your guy. Says he's a reclusive billionaire."

Claire snorted. "As if I'd sleep with a man named Maximilian. Please."

"I'd sleep with him. He invented some air-conditioning system for NASA. He's made a fortune. Too bad there aren't any pictures." She chuckled. "He likes to spend his money, though. Says here he was one of the first passengers to book his seat for Virgin Galactic's first trip to space."

"What?" Claire shrieked. "That costs two hundred grand. Let me see that." She read the biography Laurel had unearthed. Obviously the subject hadn't wanted to reveal much about himself to the public. The paragraph was vague and impersonal. She could imagine a communications person going, *Please, Maximilian, give us something interesting,* and he'd told them he was going to space.

The conversation she and Max had shared over dinner at the B and B came back to her with distressing clarity. His dream had been to go to space. She'd teased him about the cost of space tourism. And he'd dropped the subject.

"There must be pictures of him," she exclaimed. "You have to find me a picture."

Laurel's mouth dropped open. "You seriously think this might be your guy? The billionaire?"

Yes, she found, she seriously did. "So many things make sense now. How he paid for that lodge without blinking." She slapped her hands to her hot cheeks. "Oh, my God. He probably threw out the people who'd been booked in that B and B for months. Because he's a billionaire. They can do that, right? Throw around their money to get anything they want?"

"Okay. Calm down. It can't be him. Why would a billionaire named Maximilian want to come to Spruce Bay and fly as a bush pilot with Polar Air?" She glanced at her friend. "No offense."

"I don't know. But I'm going to ask him."

"Wait. Before you make a fool of yourself, let's see if we can find a photograph."

Claire waited in burning impatience while her friend clicked here and there. Finally, she said, "Okay. Here's a picture. It's not very clear. He's obviously not big on publicity."

"Let me see." She squinted at the screen. The photo had been taken at some fancy, expensive fund-raiser. The picture was from the website of the foundation. The caption read, *Lady Jane Snow-Hinton and her date for the evening, venture capitalist, Maximilian Varo.* The man in the tux was so busy talking to another man in the background that he clearly hadn't known he was being photographed—any more than she'd known when she'd been snapped at the Fourth of July party.

Even though the photo wasn't superclear, she knew it was her Max. The profile was the same, the body she knew so well was the same. Something about the way he held his head was as distinguishing to her as a fingerprint would be to a forensics expert.

"It's him."

"Oh, boy."

"But—but why? What is a venture capitalist doing at Polar Air?"

Laurel ran her fingers through her hair. It was her *I'm thinking* gesture. "They fund new enterprises, they buy ailing businesses for pennies on the dollar and turn them around, they—" But she stopped at Claire's cry of rage.

"He's planning to buy Polar Air. That's got to be it. Frank Carmondy had us mortgaged to the hilt. He must have got wind of it somehow. Planned to buy the airline for cheap." She heard her own teeth grinding. "The property alone is worth a fortune. What if he buys the mortgages? What if he forecloses?" Her voice was rising dangerously. "We'll lose everything. Everything my family has worked for. What about Lynette? Where would she go? He's planning to take our business away." She nearly choked on her own fury. "And he even slept with me to get more control."

There was a moment of silence. Fiona Apple had disappeared and some other female soloist was now singing of heartbreak and loss. Perfect!

Laurel spoke. "First, you don't know that any of this is true. He could be here for a bunch of reasons."

"Name one?"

"I don't know. But before you take a shotgun to this guy's *cojones,* you should maybe talk to him first."

"I don't like it. Why wouldn't he tell me he was rich?"

"Lots of people don't boast about their assets. Maybe he's tired of women like Lady Jane Snow-Hinton parading him around the way a big-game hunter shows off a dead lion's head. Maybe he's lost all his dough."

She snorted. "Then how could he afford the B and B?" She smacked her head. "Didn't you say that Felix

Gerard had angel investors who helped him open his place?"

Laurel nodded slowly. "What do you bet?"

"That Maximilian Varo is an angel investor? Makes sense. Felix Gerard wouldn't clear out his fancy lodge for just anyone." Her eyes narrowed as she remembered something. "When we first got there, I said, 'Are we the only guests?' And Felix looked at Max and then said, 'But of course.'"

"I agree, it does seem suspicious, but—"

"Why do we let men do this to us?" she wailed. "Why do we let them come into our perfectly happy lives and mess everything up? I was fine. We were fine." She took a breath. "Well, we had an embezzler running the operation into the ground who might, maybe, have attempted to murder me, but other than that, we were doing okay."

"And you didn't need a man."

"Exactly!" She jumped up, needing to get away from the photo of Max—no, she reminded herself—of Maximilian, and Lady Prunella Finch-Bottom or whatever her name was. "I didn't need a man. I was perfectly happy without one."

"And then he came along."

"Yes. Then he came along. And now everything's a mess."

"I'm not siding with him, you know I'm not, but it did sound like he was a good guy to have along when your plane went down."

She swung around. "I would have survived by myself." She thought of the way Max had risked his life to grab the survival kit, and how nice it had been not to be alone in that ordeal. But even so, she was pretty sure she'd have made it back alive.

"I admit it was nice to have company. I wouldn't have enjoyed going through that alone." She wasn't saying she'd enjoyed the ordeal with Max, either, but it had been less terrible than it could have been.

She paced a little. Then she asked Laurel, "Can he buy the business without our consent?"

Laurel ran her fingers through her hair again. She was starting to look slightly wild. "I'm not sure. It depends who holds the mortgages and if they'd sell them. It depends on how deeply Polar Air is in debt. Do you know?"

She blew out a breath. "It's bad. I trusted Frank. We all did. Since I found out he was stealing from us, I've been studying the books, trying to follow the money." She faced her friend. "I've hired an accounting firm to try and sort out the mess, but it's not good."

"Look. Maximilian Varo's a venture capitalist. Maybe you can make a deal with him. Get him to help you."

"If he was interested in helping us, wouldn't he have been up front about who he was and why he was here?"

Laurel looked as though she wished she'd never suggested the Google search. It was as though they'd gone to a fortune-teller giggling and figuring they'd both find out they were going to inherit money and marry dark, handsome strangers, only to find out that their futures were going to be bleak and tragic.

"I was so stupid. First I trusted Frank. Then Max."

Now she wondered if she could ever trust her own judgment again.

"You can't be blamed for Frank. Your grandparents hired him."

"Well, I hired Max."

"Okay. That one's on you."

"I should go. Thanks for dinner."

Laurel said, "Let me ask you one more thing. Do you love him?"

She closed her eyes for a moment and then opened them. "I can't answer that question because I do not want to hear the words that might come out of my mouth."

"So, that's a yes, then."

With a strangled cry, she headed for the door.

19

CLAIRE WAS GLAD she was on a bike, she had such a mad on the ride was good for her. She pushed through her anger by jamming down hard on the pedals until she was flying along the road. She was gasping for breath when she reached the Polar Air property.

Max's cabin was dark when she pulled up in front of it. She checked her watch but it wasn't late, barely 9:30. She leaned her bike against the front porch. Banged on his door.

Nothing.

She called and still nothing. Was he out in town?

Finally, she rode back toward her own place and as she passed the lockup for the planes, she noticed that Max's wasn't there. She pedaled as though a fire-breathing monster was after her, got to Lynette's and fishtailed when she tried to stop. She dropped her bike just like she had when she was a little kid, simply left it lying on the gravel and pounded up the stairs. She ran into her grandmother's house.

"Grandma? Lynette?"

"I'm watching TV."

When she burst into the room, Lynette adjusted her glasses. "Claire?" she said. "What is it?"

"Where's Max?"

"He had to go down south. Said there was something important he had to deal with. He'll be back in a couple of days."

"A couple of days?" she cried. She sat down. Stood up. The characters on *Glee* continued to sing their harmonic hearts out on the TV. "A couple of days?"

"Claire. What is it?"

She threw back her head, a wolf in midhowl. "Men!"

The *Glee* cast got cut off midnote.

"All men or one in particular?" The older woman's voice was puzzled and perhaps a touch amused.

"It's Max. I'm really sorry to tell you this, Grandma. But I don't think he's who he says he is."

"Well, who is? The longer you live the more you realize that most of us are living in a fantasy of our own creation." She snorted. "Have you ever read personal ads? If the people were as fantastic as they say they are, they'd never be single in the first place."

"That's exaggeration. This is downright lying."

"Sit down, honey. You're giving me a crick in my neck. Then tell me all about it calmly."

Calmly? Right now Claire didn't have a calm molecule in her body.

Still, she drew a full breath, held on to it for a few seconds and then slowly let it out. Then she told Lynette everything Laurel and she had found out about Max.

"So, his name's Maximilian. Well, you can't blame a man for hiding that."

"It's not the name, Lynette. It's everything else that goes with the name."

"Like that he's a bazillionaire."

"A bazillionaire masquerading as a bush pilot."

"I don't think he is. You can't hide that kind of thing. He's got the skills and he's logged the hours flying. We checked his references and his credentials."

"But why is he here?"

"Why is anyone here?"

She let out an infuriated cry. "I don't mean in an existential way, I mean why, specifically, is Maximilian Varo, owner of a venture-capital firm that buys struggling companies for cheap and turns them around, here?"

"I don't know. But even if our Max is this Maximilian person, the fact that he's here doesn't mean he's up to no good." She sighed. "We used to trust people. We used to take them at their word. We still don't lock our doors at night. Spruce Bay isn't that kind of town. Never has been. And we're not that kind of people."

"But—"

"I'm as sorry as I can be that Frank Carmondy went down the path he did. But he's paid for it with his life. And of all the people I've trusted in my life, and I've been around for a lot of years, he's the only one who's ever let me down."

"But—"

"He's let you down, too. I know that. And badly. Frank was a trusted employee, more like family, really. And he betrayed that trust. But that doesn't mean we don't extend trust to others."

"But why, why would Max be here if it wasn't to take our business away?"

"I don't know. But it seems to me if he's as much of a big shot as you say he is that he'd have underlings buying up no-account airlines. What's he doing here himself?"

That was the part she still didn't understand. "I don't know."

"Well, maybe we should ask him before we get ourselves too riled up."

"I would ask him," she said with forced patience, "but he's not here. He's gone south on some mysterious errand."

"What do you think he's going to do?"

"I don't know. Laurel's the one with the business degree. She talked about hostile takeovers and buying up mortgages for pennies on the dollar. I think, since Frank helped himself to the cash drawer, that we are vulnerable."

Lynette rose. She came closer and rubbed Claire's shoulder. "Polar Air has been around for a long time. We've survived terrible weather, economic downturn, competition from other airlines." Her face creased for a second. "We lost our only child to a foolish car accident. You lost your parents. I lost my husband. And we've always survived. Sure, we're weakened right now and hurting, but whatever happens, I think we'll make it."

"I wish I had your optimism."

"I wish you did, too. You'd be a lot happier."

HE WAS GOING to tell her, Max decided as his plane drew closer to Spruce Bay. He felt anticipation building inside him. He was going to see Claire again. Kiss Claire again. Make love to Claire again.

He felt as though he hadn't seen her for weeks when it had only been a couple of days.

He wondered how she'd react when she discovered who he really was.

Once more he was reminded of *The Prince and the Pauper* where the poor guy turns out to be pretty flush with cash. He could finally remove the crease of worry between Claire's pretty hazel eyes. He wanted to take some of the burden off her shoulders more than he could ever remember wanting anything.

If the fairy tale held true, he'd discovered a woman who loved him for himself. For the bone-deep qualities he believed he possessed and not for his material possessions, especially his money, which had come to him more as a fluke than anything else.

It helped that she loved to fly as much as he did, that she was adventurous and loving and that they fit together so well, whether in bed or in conversation over coffee and the paper. He imagined having children with her, flying to remote spots and camping out with her, growing old with her.

He let out a breath. Oh, yeah. He was a goner.

Looked like Dylan was going to win their foolish bet after all.

He'd never lost anything more willingly.

When he landed, he felt a smile begin to bloom. He grabbed his bag and the bouquet of roses he'd picked up in Seattle because they'd looked so fresh, the way flowers should look. The only place in Spruce Bay that had flower arrangements was the grocery store, and the couple of times he'd gone by the blooms had looked like they had died and somebody'd glued the petals back on. Saddest damn things he'd ever seen.

He liked to give a woman flowers. And Claire seemed like a woman who should receive roses on a regular basis.

Specifically from him.

When he jumped down from the plane he strode off in the direction of the office, hoping to catch her on the ground. He'd tried to rehearse what he wanted to say to her on the flight up, but he didn't want it to sound like a speech, nor did he want to come across as some arrogant twit so full of himself that he thought a few bucks would make a difference in their relationship. Still, as Adam's fiancée had reminded him during his brief visit home, there came a point when a woman deserved full disclosure. He suspected he'd reached that point, especially since he wanted to help her save her family company.

He knew the second Claire saw him. In fact, it seemed almost as though she'd been waiting for him. The outer door of the office building flew open and she pretty much ran toward him.

It felt like that moment in the movies or TV commercials when the lovers run toward each other, usually barefoot and on the beach. They may not have been on a beach, but he was pretty sure the handful of roses he was holding out went a long way in the romance department.

It wasn't until she got closer that he noticed the expression on her face.

It wasn't the bliss of a woman about to embrace her lover.

Looked more like the grim mask of an executioner as he raised the ax.

He stopped in midstride, puzzled. "Hey, is everything okay?"

She'd sprinted so hard she was out of breath. Her eyes snapped with fury. "No. Everything's not okay, *Maximilian!*" She pretty much spat out the formal version of his name. Funny how when he heard himself called that, it often meant somebody was mad at him. Usually, his mom.

It seemed, based on Claire's use of his full name, that she had probably figured out who he was.

And she didn't seem thrilled.

She stood there in front of him, her hands wrapped firmly around her torso. He got the impression that she was holding them tight to prevent herself from slapping his face or punching him or something.

They weren't even alone. Lynette had emerged from the office right behind Claire, walking at a normal pace, and had nearly reached them. One other pilot was walking up toward the office, and a maintenance guy was looking over at them with interest.

Max felt foolish standing there with roses in one hand and his flight bag in the other. Clearly, she wasn't going to take the flowers. It seemed equally obvious, based on her expression, that they were about to have a heated discussion.

Max figured a guy who could invent a climate-control system for spaceships ought to be able to manage to have a private conversation without unwanted roses in his hand.

So, when Lynette drew close enough, he said, "Could you take these?" and thrust the flowers into her hand.

Lynette didn't look as hostile as her granddaughter, which was good, but she didn't seem like she was altogether thrilled to see him, either. He figured he'd deal with the granddaughter first, then talk to Lynette.

"Can I talk to you privately?" he said to Claire.

"I don't want to talk to you. I don't even know who you are."

He gave her a look, the look of a man who's been inside a woman's body and shared the most intimate experience possible with her. She could say whatever she liked, but on the most basic level they knew each other.

Her color rose slightly. Seemed her thoughts had gone along the same path.

"Let's go for a walk. I'll tell you everything you want to know."

20

"I want to know why you lied to us."

"I never lied to you," he said.

She snorted. "Not telling the truth is pretty much the same thing as lying."

He started walking, not sure if she'd join him but completely certain he didn't want an audience for this conversation. To his relief she did follow, stomping along at his side. She didn't ask where they were going, merely started a rant that had clearly been boiling up for a while. "I was at my friend Laurel's place. She did a Google search on you. I can't even tell you how I felt, how, how, betrayed I felt when I found out who you really are. What are you doing here?"

"I—"

"Why didn't you tell me?"

He got close enough to his place to toss his flight bag onto the front porch and then, feeling a little more in control with both hands free, started guiding them in the direction of the path that ran along the headlands above the ocean. He loved it there, loved watching the endless, restless waves. He found it soothing and very much hoped his irate companion did, too.

He let her continue her tirade, knowing there was no point trying to stop her. Clearly she had things she needed to say to him.

When she stopped to take a breath, he turned to her and said, "I only have one thing to say."

She turned to him, crossed her arms. "What?"

"I love you."

If he thought those magic words would have her opening her tightly crossed arms and throwing them around him, he was sadly mistaken. The thing was, he'd never said those words to any woman but his mom. Maybe his sister on a birthday card. He wasn't a person who threw out deep sentiments like cheap candy. It was hard to say them. Even now, he felt as though he'd taken a huge risk. Breathing felt like something he had to concentrate on. He'd actually said *I love you*.

"If you love me, why did you lie to me?"

"I—" No point in saying he hadn't lied. In her eyes, omission of information was the same as a lie. And he supposed there was some evasion of the truth in what he'd done.

He thought about what Dylan had said. "Do you ever watch a show called *Undercover Boss?*"

She glanced at him with scorn. "No."

"Well, it's a reality show where the boss goes incognito into—"

"You're not my boss."

"Right, but the point is—"

"You are my employee. And it seems to me that you have, in fact, been acting as a corporate spy."

"Look, Varo Enterprises doesn't need—"

"Then why did you come here? You clearly don't need a job as a bush pilot."

He let out a breath. Stared out at the ocean and thought

about that very question. Why had he come? "I think I was bored. No. I know I was bored. Everything was working too well, too smoothly. I need challenges. I have more money than I can ever spend, employees who are so amazing nobody needs me for anything except to approve their excellent decisions and sign some deals. Polar Air came up as a possible turnaround or buyout." He shrugged.

"I'm sorry, Claire. People talk. There were rumors that bills weren't being paid and the airline was in trouble." He rubbed a spot on his forehead as though it would ease his thought process. "This is a tiny deal for us, obviously, but we liked the reputation of your airline and its strategic location. We could link up with some other interests and maximize economies of scale. Maybe get a regional airline going. Lots of options."

"Except the option of talking to us first."

"Look, we aren't bad people. We don't do hostile takeovers and put people out of business. But there was obviously something going wrong. The project manager suggested it would be nice to have eyes and ears on the ground, just to get an idea of what was going on before we committed ourselves."

"So you sent in a corporate spy." She still seemed pretty pissed. "You."

He blew out a breath that was immediately carried away by the breeze, the way he felt his hopes for the future were going.

"I can see why it could look that way to you." In fact, when she phrased it that way it looked sort of like corporate espionage to him, too. What the hell had he been thinking?

He took one look at her angry face and knew he had to think fast. He had a genius brain, didn't he? Some of the best education money could buy. How could he not come up with a reasonable answer for why he'd chosen to come to Alaska and fly bush planes?

And then he knew. "I love to fly. I was born for it. I've loved the idea of space travel ever since I was a geek." He caught her expression and amended his statement. "A younger geek than I am now. I know this sounds stupid but I feel like I belong in the air. You know how some people love to swim and sail and scuba dive, and others are tethered to the earth, they hike and climb and garden. But for me, I've always felt most at home in the sky. I should have been a bird."

He caught the sympathetic look that crossed her face and knew, as he'd known from the very beginning, that she felt exactly the same way. Of course, she wasn't going to say so since she was currently steaming mad at him, but he knew she understood in a way few people did.

"That's probably when I started falling in love with you, when I realized you were also born to fly." He found, now that he'd said it once, throwing out the *love* word was getting easier. Or maybe it was simple desperation driving him.

Losing Claire would be right up there with finding out he could never be an astronaut. A dream buster, a life changer, a blow that would be extremely difficult to recover from.

"I came here to check out the airline from the inside, it's true, but never with any malicious intent. I didn't want to raise false hopes. If I liked the operation, I was planning to get my company to make you a fair offer."

"What if we don't want to sell?"

This was more difficult. He'd met with his people in Seattle and he knew, probably better than Claire, that Polar Air was in serious financial trouble. Sure, it was the fault of the former manager, but now that he was dead, it was unlikely they'd ever get any of their money back. And even if they did, it wouldn't come fast enough. He gentled his voice. "I think you're going to have to consider selling. Or getting an angel investor."

"Angel investor seems like one of those—what is that term for when you put two words together that don't belong?"

"Oxymoron."

"Right. I don't think someone who gives us money in order to control our business is much of an angel, frankly."

"But you do see that you're in a tough spot? Through no fault of your own," he hastened to add. "Frank Carmondy was stealing from you, taking money that should have gone to suppliers, so you thought everything was paid up. And because Polar Air has such a great reputation, suppliers were willing to wait longer to get paid."

"They trusted us." She looked sad and angry. "They trusted Polar Air because my grandmother and grandfather are the kind of people who'd deprive themselves to make sure all their bills were paid on time." She looked out to sea. Her profile was beautiful, he thought. "This is going to be so hard for Lynette."

"Look, I want to make a suggestion."

When she turned back to him her eyes were hard. "I don't think so, Max. Whatever it is, I don't want to hear it. What I want you to do is pack your bags and get back on your plane and go back to your fancy office and your billions. You've had your fun slumming it, you got to ride toy planes, now you need to go back to your real life."

"But—"

"Really. You need to go."

He could see that she was fighting emotion and as much as he wanted to pull her into his arms and kiss her until she could see reason, could see what was in his heart, he knew he couldn't do that.

If she wanted him to leave, he was going to have to leave.

"WHERE'S MAX?" Lynette asked when Claire came stomping into the house.

"He's gone."

"He just got back. Now where's he gone to?"

"Back to Seattle, I guess. I fired him."

Lynette didn't act shocked or even surprised. Instead, she fussed with the roses. She'd put them in a pretty crystal vase that her husband had given her on one of their anniversaries. "He brought roses."

"He came here under false pretenses and he wanted to buy Polar Air."

"Well, at least he's got good taste."

"How can you say that?"

Her grandmother ruffled her hair the way she'd done when she was a teenager. "Because he also wants you."

"It was probably a ruse. Get close to me and get closer to stealing our airline."

"So young and so cynical."

"Lynette, you are not taking this seriously."

"At my age, honey, you learn to take everything less seriously. And maybe I'm old enough to understand that everything isn't as black-and-white as it seemed when I was as young as you are."

"He lied to us."

"Well, he didn't tell us exactly who he was or why he was here, but I'm not sure he actually lied."

"Are you on his side? Just because he flew in some damned roses?"

"No. I'm not on his side. But I think a man who is smart enough to love my granddaughter must have some redeeming features. What was his offer?"

Claire was so shocked she took a step back. "He didn't offer me anything. And if he did I wouldn't—"

"Not you. I meant, what was his offer for Polar Air?"

"I have no idea. I told you, I fired him."

"Hmm. Might have been interesting to find out what he was offering."

"But—you'd never sell the family business. You started the airline."

"No. I don't plan to sell. But I'm a businesswoman. Best way to gauge the value of your business is to find out what someone else is willing to pay for it."

CLAIRE HEADED to the ice rink. With the frame of mind she was in, pucks were going to be punished tonight. She went an hour early so she could practice with the Spruce Bay Vixens, the team she'd played for from her senior high school years to her mid-twenties. The team always welcomed her at practice. She enjoyed the other young women and was able to give a few coaching pointers.

After the girls hit the showers, she remained on the ice alone. She still hadn't skated her mad off. She tried not to picture the way she and Max had faced off on this very rink. How they'd toyed with each other and challenged each other and enjoyed a crazy kind of courtship on the ice.

She'd recruited the Vixens' goalie to come out and try to stop her shots. She lined up pucks. Every time she focused, she imagined the puck had his face on it and was saying, "I love you." Then she'd whack that sucker so hard the poor goalie didn't have a chance.

They were both breathing hard and she had an ache in her shooting arm when they called it quits.

"Nice work," she said to the goalie, whose name was Jennifer.

"I barely stopped half your shots."

"I know. If you can stop half my shots, you're doing okay."

The younger woman took a pull from her water bottle and wiped her sweaty forehead with her arm. "I guess so. You're pretty famous around here. How come you didn't go to the Olympics?"

She remembered the heady days when she'd imagined playing hockey for her country. She'd been so excited. As had Lynette and her grandfather.

She was still happy that he'd been around to get the news. He'd been so proud he'd called his travel agent and booked tickets right then and there for Lynette and him to fly to Turin for the 2006 winter Olympics.

He'd died before the tickets could be delivered. Lynette hadn't fallen apart. And she hadn't even hinted that Claire should miss her chance at glory and stay home. But she'd known that her grandmother was holding herself together with determination and chewing gum. And Claire had stayed to help her run the airline and to grieve.

There were moments when she thought maybe, just maybe, if she'd been part of the women's Olympic hockey team the Canadians wouldn't have had such an easy victory. But she also knew in her heart that her grandfather would have given her a gold medal for doing the right thing.

And that was worth more than Olympic gold. Her

grandparents had taken her in when she was a grief-stricken teenager and they'd helped her through her sadness, anger and confusion. She found, when the time came, it was an easy decision to return the favor to her grandmother.

"My grandfather died. I needed to stay home."

"You missed the Olympics. That blows."

"Not as much as losing my grandfather."

"Yeah," said the worldly wise eighteen-year-old. "Sometimes life just sucks."

She thought of Max off in some boardroom buying up airlines as though they were penny candy before escorting Lady Prunella Pink-eye Jones to some charity event. "Yeah," she agreed. "Sometimes life completely sucks."

21

THE *SPRUCE BAY SENTINEL* was published on Thursdays.

The paper didn't bother with world or national news since everyone had satellite TV and read the big papers online. Instead, the *Sentinel* focused on Spruce Bay, which the *New York Times* and *USA TODAY* and network news almost never did. Once, they'd gained notoriety because an escaped murderer had turned up in town, eaten at Peg's Diner, which had been closed now for more than a decade, and been arrested after spending a night at the Inn.

If the murderer hadn't used the victim's credit card all over town, he might never have been apprehended.

Since then, Spruce Bay had dropped off the news map. So the *Sentinel* filled in the gaps. This was the paper that everyone in town read. It was the place to find vitriolic exchanges in the letters-to-the-editor section. Where road closures were news. As were social events. Births and deaths got pretty big coverage. Family weddings were news, as were stories about the children and grandchildren who'd left (most of them) to pursue life elsewhere.

Frank Carmondy's death and Claire and Max's airline crash had created a news bonanza the paper hadn't seen for some time. Since she had no interest in reading about either one, Claire had avoided looking at the *Sentinel* this morning. It was almost a week since she'd fired Max. He hadn't bothered to contact her or her grandmother, though she woke every morning wondering if this was the day Varo Enterprises would attempt a takeover.

She was on her way to the grocery store the first time she was stopped. "So? You going?" Albert Fonse asked her.

Albert operated a menswear store with a barbershop in the back. He was outside enjoying the sunshine since, presumably, he didn't have any customers.

"Going where?"

Instead of answering, he broke into laughter. "Oh, missy. I'm getting a ringside seat, I'll tell you that."

Wondering if Albert had been in the sun too long, she nodded politely and moved on.

In the grocery store, the strange behavior continued. People she barely knew pointed at her and whispered. There were giggles and when Pearl Nahanee rang up her order, she said, "Sure is a lot of excitement about the big game."

Once more, she nodded. Claire didn't always keep up on all the local sports. No doubt the Elks were having a bonspiel and she'd forgotten.

With her grocery sacks stowed in the Yukon, she stopped by the Inn on impulse. It was three in the afternoon, a quiet time. Laurel was supervising a couple of busboys who'd been hauled out of the kitchen to wash windows. But when she saw Claire, she said, "I'll be back in a half hour. I better not find any streaks. And I want all those cobwebs gone, too."

Then she grabbed Claire's arm and dragged her down the hall to her office.

"Oh, my God. I was going to drive over to your place as soon as I got off work. I can't believe you didn't call me right away. The suspense is killing me. Are you going to do it?"

"Do what? Everybody is acting so weird today. What's going on?"

"You mean you haven't seen it?"

"I don't think so."

Laurel looked like she was trying with all her might not to laugh. There was a telltale dent in her cheek that suggested she was biting the inside of her mouth to control some kind of bottled-up hilarity.

Laurel wasn't given to uncontrolled mirth, so Claire said, "What?"

Laurel grabbed a copy of the *Sentinel,* which would have been published that very day, and pushed it at her.

She glanced up and back down. "I know I was interviewed after the crash. I don't want to read it."

Laurel shook her head. "It's not that."

"Tell me now, is it another embarrassing candid photo? I survived three days in the bush. Give me a break."

"Just open the paper. To page three."

She opened the paper. The front page had the photograph of her and Max getting off the rescue chopper. On page two was a photo of Frank and a big write-up. She knew Lynette had been interviewed and, of course, had been gracious about the man.

But it wasn't the long obituary that caught her eye. It was the big, full-page ad staring her in the face when she turned to page three.

A full-page ad.

And it said:

Max Varo, CEO of Varo Enterprises, Inc., wishes
to acquire control of Polar Air Ltd.
Mr. Varo challenges Ms. Claire Lundstrom to a
one-on-one hockey game to be played next Fri-
day night at the Spruce Bay Arena.
Admission Free.
Public welcome.
Game starts at 7:00 p.m. sharp.

THERE WAS SILENCE in the room but for the crinkle of
newspaper as she stared at the ad.

"He's crazy," she said at last.

"As a bedbug."

"You can't play one-on-one hockey. There's no such
thing."

"Really? I didn't know that."

"You can go one-on-one in basketball. Not hockey.
Anyway, I can't play hockey with Max to decide who
gets Polar Air. It's ridiculous."

"Can you beat him?"

"Of course I can beat him."

"Does he know you were drafted for the Olympics?"

"No. But I've practiced with him. He's seen me
skate."

"Has he seen your A game?"

"We were doing drills. Like I said, you can't play a
hockey game with two people."

"Then what's the problem? I think you should do it."

"Is it even legal? You can't buy a company based on
a hockey game."

"Seems to me, people gamble with businesses all
the time. So long as Lynette agrees, I think you can."

She gnawed her lip, thinking. "Do you think we'll
have an audience?"

Laurel did the biting her cheek thing again, and then said, "Yeah. I think you'll have an audience." She glanced at Claire and the paper and choked on a half-suppressed giggle. "Honey, everybody in town is talking about the big game. It's the most exciting thing that's happened around here in years." She paused and then said, "Well, that didn't involve some kind of act of God. Or grizzlies."

"You're asking me to show up at a crowded rink and humiliate Max so that I can save our family business?"

"Seems to me he's asking to be humiliated. He's a big boy. He can take it. He'll simply fly out of here again and pay people big bucks to soothe his ego."

She paced the small office. Laurel watched but didn't say a word.

"Oh, I am so tempted."

"He has no idea how good you are, does he?"

"None at all."

"Do it."

"He said he loves me."

"Oh, he needs to be punished. Nail him with a well-placed puck."

"You're right, I will."

"MAX, DUDE, YOU can't have a one-on-one hockey tournament with a girl," Dylan told him when he explained to his two friends why he was currently back in Hunter with his tail between his legs. The one good thing about being home was he'd been able to make a practice with the Hunter Hurricanes.

The three were alone in the change room now that the rest of the team had left. Max was zipping up his hockey bag.

"You can't play one-on-one hockey at all," Adam

chimed in. "Doesn't even make sense. You could challenge her to basketball one-on-one, but you suck at basketball."

"Would you guys trust me? Anyhow, I can't back down now. I've already put an ad in the paper."

"Why couldn't you fly up to Alaska and have a meeting in a boardroom like a normal person?"

"Because I'm not trying to buy an airline. I'm trying to win back the woman I love."

"By beating her ass at hockey in front of everybody in the town where she lives? This is your plan to win her back?" Dylan was rubbing his hair with a towel after his postpractice shower.

Okay, when he put it like that it didn't sound like the greatest plan in history. But they didn't know Claire. He did. Or at least he liked to think he did. Although, if he'd really understood her, he'd have told her much earlier that he wasn't only a bush pilot. That he had simply wanted to spend time flying and enjoying a different kind of life. That sometimes he got tired of suits and meetings and all the assorted crap that could seriously undermine how cool it was to be in his position. He had kept his feelings to himself, as he always did, not wanting to come across as a poor little rich boy.

"Yep. It's my plan."

"Is there a backup plan? A plan B?"

In the silence he could hear the drip of water coming from the shower area, which pretty much answered the question.

"You are so screwed."

"Okay, then. Wish me luck."

Adam made a derisive sound. "We're your best friends and your teammates. We're not letting you play the hockey game of your life without us there to cheer you on. You got room for three more in your plane?"

"Three more? You bringing along a doctor in case she takes me out?"

"No, dummy. We're bringing Serena. She's a performance coach. Maybe she can help you avoid making a fool of yourself."

"Might be too late for that," Dylan said, pulling on a T-shirt so wrinkled Max could hardly stand to watch. "Have you heard from Claire?"

"No." And it was worrying him. He'd expected a phone call from Claire, had been glued to his cell ever since he'd put the ad in the paper. But nothing. "What if she doesn't show up?"

"You'll have a shiny fresh rink you've paid for. Me and Adam will get in some much-needed practice time with you."

Max shot him a look.

Dylan put up his hands. "Hey, I like to look on the bright side."

Adam regarded him. "Don't you want him to work things out with Claire so you win the Last Bachelor Standing bet?"

Dylan's grin was infectious. "See what I love about this situation? I can't lose!"

22

THE DAY OF THE hockey tournament came a lot faster than Claire's decision on whether she was going to show up or not. To answer his summons, in fact.

When she woke up, she was surprised to find she had been asleep at all. Most of the night she'd tossed and fretted and watched the clock tick the seconds, the minutes, the hours. It felt like she waffled with each tick. Show up at the rink? Play the kind of hockey that had won her a spot on the Olympic team? Pound puck after puck past an astonished Max until he was so humiliated that he called it quits?

In her meanest moments she sort of relished the image of him, sprawled on the ice, sweating and panting and begging her to stop. But she didn't want to humiliate the man in public, even if he had brought the fight to her.

She wanted—and then she'd have to toss around again for a bit, trying to find a comfortable spot in her lonely bed—she wanted what exactly? For him to go away and never come back?

Yes. Sort of.

But she wanted to make sure he clearly understood

how much he'd hurt and betrayed her. She needed to
see him again just so she could tell him that. And then
he could go away and never come back.

She'd toss a little more while her restless renegade
of a body longed for his strong arms around her, for the
low mumble of his voice when they talked late into the
night, long after they'd made love.

Oh, she missed him. No, she reminded herself,
punching the pillow to get it into the right shape, she
did not miss Maximilian Varo, billionaire aerospace
brainiac, she missed Max. Her Max, the guy who flew
Beavers and Cessnas and made terrible coffee.

That last thought had her sitting bolt upright. Of
course he made terrible coffee. He had staff. Nobody with his money made their own coffee. If only
she hadn't been so foolishly, crazily in love with him,
she'd have seen the telltale signs that he was really a
rich tycoon.

The signs were all around her.

He couldn't make coffee.

He…well, he couldn't make coffee.

She pulled her knees up to her chest and plunked her
much-abused pillow behind her back while she contemplated all the ways Max had slipped up, revealing his
spoiled rich-boy status.

Well, she thought, that was easy. This wasn't Sea-
Tac Airport; at Polar Air the pilots also washed and
cleaned the planes. He'd…she leaned back against the
wall and hit her head. "Ow." She drew up a picture of
Max out there hosing down the plane, joking with—in
her mental picture she couldn't pull up the second person. All her attention had been on Max, with his dark
good looks, his white, white smile and the neat and tidy
way he went about completing a messy job.

Okay, so he could wash a plane without acting like it was beneath him. But there were other signs, other signs she should have picked up on.

"Aha," she said aloud, suddenly remembering the truck he'd bought when he first started with Polar Air. She groaned inwardly as she recalled how she'd worried about where the money had come from. And he'd said, what had he said? Something that reassured her? Some lie.

She thought back. He'd said...now she remembered as clearly as though he were in her bedroom repeating the words. He'd said, "Don't worry. I have money." Something like that, but of course she'd assumed they were talking human scale amounts.

And wasn't that the understatement of the year. She'd taken him at his word because she'd liked him even then and he'd seemed like an honest man. How he must have been laughing at her inside.

Her blood didn't boil, exactly, but she was fairly certain it heated up a degree or two. Had he been laughing at them the whole time? These Alaskan rubes who wouldn't know a billionaire from a snow shovel?

She banged her head back against the wall a couple more times until she realized she'd need an aspirin if she didn't stop.

But round and round she went. Go and face off with this guy in a public rink for a stupid game you couldn't even play one-on-one? Were they going to pull teams from thin air? Or should she do the sensible thing and simply refuse to play?

Coffee didn't help. The granola and yogurt and fruit she forced herself to eat didn't help.

When she headed out to the office she found two of the pilots and their maintenance guy in low conversation. Cash quickly disappeared off the tabletop and the three guys dispersed like a gang under surveillance.

"What's going on?" she asked, drilling them with her eyes.

"Nothing."

Nobody would meet her gaze.

"What kind of nothing?"

Finally, the maintenance guy said, "You going to play tonight or what? I got ten that says you go for it. I'm thinking of raising my bet to twenty."

She could only stare. Finally she found her voice. "You are betting on whether I'll play hockey against Max tonight?"

"Yeah." And he looked at her expectantly.

"Much as I'd like to help you win some money, I can't. I don't know."

She walked into the office, realized she was worse than useless, walked out again.

"If you need me, I'll be at Lynette's." And she walked out with as much dignity as a person can knowing her staff have a betting pool going on her.

When she opened Lynette's front door and called out, her grandmother's voice came from the kitchen. "Figured you'd be by. Coffee's fresh. And I baked morning-glory muffins."

She didn't have to announce that they were Claire's favorite, obviously, but the words hung silently in the air.

Morning-glory muffins were also part of the breakfast of champions that she'd always eaten the morning of a big game. With a mental groan, Claire realized that granola, fruit and yogurt had also been a part of that morning routine. Then she'd have a huge, protein-packed meal at midday, followed by an energy snack before the game.

She entered the kitchen and Lynette handed her a mug of coffee. The muffins were already sitting on the table, steaming away in a basket. "I got eggs if you want them."

"No, thanks. Muffin's good."

She sat at the table. She might be mad at Max and she might be seriously considering leaving him all alone at center ice in full view of the entire town of citizens he'd hoodwinked, but that didn't mean she wasn't going to eat one of her favorite muffins.

She reached for one, still warm from the oven, tore it open and spread the treat lavishly with butter.

When she bit in she started to feel better.

She tasted carrot and raisins and a hint of cinnamon. Knew there was oatmeal and good things inside that muffin, but what it tasted like to her was family loyalty.

Lynette had her back.

Her mouth was full when her grandmother sat opposite her, helped herself to one of the muffins and said, "Well? You going to meet that foolish young man on the ice?"

"You just cut right to the chase, don't you, Grandma?"

"I don't see the point in wasting time. At my age, I don't have much to waste."

"I've been awake half the night trying to figure out the answer to that question."

Lynette nodded. Sipped her coffee. "He'll look pretty foolish standing out there all on his own at center ice while every single person in town stares at him."

"Oh, come on. Not every single person."

"Well, Jamie-Lynn Burton says if her contractions get any closer together she won't be there, but she's hoping it's only false labor. And of course, if she has the baby during the game then Doc Bouton will have to go deliver it. Other than that, I think you can count on every breathing soul between the ages of four and dead showing up at the rink."

She'd known there were people who'd come, of course, her friends, a few of the curious who had nothing better to do on a Friday night, but everybody? "Why do people care so much? He's trying to get control of Polar Air. That's all he wants."

"Is it?"

The sound that came out of her mouth was surprisingly like a growl.

She ripped open another muffin, stuffed half in her mouth.

"What do you want, honey?"

"I want—" And there was the problem that had kept her awake half the night. She didn't know what she wanted. "I want to go back to before, when he was a bush pilot and we..."

"Fell in love," Lynette finished for her.

"Well, one of us did."

Lynette didn't reply, simply sat, ate her muffin and drank her coffee. Slowly Claire began to feel less hysterical and more centered. "What do you think I should do?"

"It's not my decision. It's yours."

She hated it when Lynette did that. "I know it's my decision, but if you were in my place and you had to make it, what would you do?"

"I guess that would depend on whether I wanted to fight for what I want."

"Of course I want to fight. I'll fight anybody to keep

Polar Air. It's our family's business. It's who we are. What we do."

Lynette had a half smile on her face. "Well, then."

"Well, then." She sighed. "I guess I'm going to play hockey tonight."

"First time you've played a public game in a while. How are your skills?"

"Rusty, but I can still whup his ass."

"That's my girl."

"You coming?"

Her grandmother wiped her mouth with a napkin before replying. "Oh, yes. I'll be there."

"You know, you don't have to."

"Actually, I do." She didn't look at Claire but fiddled with her coffee mug. "Ted Lowenbrau phoned me."

"If he's part of this ridiculous betting pool I hope you told him where to get off."

"No. That's not why he called, though I believe he has a fifty that says you'll show up at the rink. Ted's always liked you."

"Then why did he call you?"

"They've asked me to referee."

23

THERE WAS ENOUGH keyed-up excitement in the Spruce Bay rink that night to make the NHL jealous, Claire thought as she made her way from the change room. She'd chosen to wear her Vixens uniform as a reminder that she was part of the fabric of this town in the same way Polar Air was. And Max had better remember that.

These were her people and this was her town.

Lynette hadn't lied. Everyone from the mayor to infants in arms piled into the seats. She noted some last-minute betting and could only assume the betting pool had moved on to the thorny question of who would win this impromptu match.

Well, everyone in town knew her history so she doubted the betting was very spirited. It was pretty much a foregone conclusion that an Olympian could kick the butt of a civilian.

Ted Lowenbrau was the announcer for the evening, a job he'd been doing for years. "Good evening, ladies and gentlemen," he said into the mic. "Tonight we are privileged to watch a very special hockey game that will decide the fate of our beloved Polar Air. Fighting for her family's company is our hometown girl, Claire Lundstrom!"

She skated onto the ice to thunderous applause. As she spun in a circle, acknowledging the packed stands, she saw Laurel waving and blowing a kiss her way. As she looked around she realized that these were her friends, her coworkers, her neighbors, her townspeople. She wasn't about to let them down.

While she acknowledged the crowd Ted went through her accomplishments from winning MVP for the Vixens three years running to being scouted for the Olympic hockey team. She hoped Max was listening.

To her surprise, she saw Felix Gerard sitting not far from Laurel. He blew her a kiss. She nodded her head slightly, knowing he was probably here for Max.

Jamie-Lynn Burton sat near the center line and to Claire's eyes she didn't seem all that comfortable. She seemed to be squirming on her seat and kind of huffing when she breathed. To Claire's relief, she noticed that Doc Bouton was sitting only a few seats away.

The few people she didn't recognize had to be Max's fancy friends from down south. Two men, almost as good-looking as Max himself, and sandwiched between them an elegant-looking woman who immediately made Claire feel bulky and sweaty in her hockey uniform.

When she caught the woman's eye, she could have sworn the woman winked at her. No doubt it was a trick of the light.

"And now," the announcer boomed, "the man who is here tonight to battle for the right to buy our own, homegrown airline, Polar Air. Max Varo."

If the applause for Max wasn't the thunderstorm Claire had experienced, it was fairly respectable. She'd almost expected hissing and booing but it seemed folks were willing to give him a chance. Or they were unwilling to piss off the guy who might soon own the only airline that could fly them in and out of town.

When he stepped onto the ice, her foolish heart skipped a beat. Max also did a circle, acknowledging the crowd. Ted reminded the crowd that Max had been working and living among them as a bush pilot for Polar Air. "But he's also a fine hockey player who plays for the Hunter Hurricanes in Hunter, Washington. The Hurricanes have won silver two years in a row at the Badges on Ice tournament, a charity tourney for the emergency-services leagues."

Max wore his Hunter Hurricanes uniform. She wondered how they'd come to the point where they were facing off on two very different teams.

She was keyed up, ready to play, when the announcer said, "And now, please rise for our national anthem, performed by the Spruce Bay High School band with vocalist Tamsin Milner."

What the…?

She glanced at Max and found him grinning with amusement. The Spruce Bay High School band had never seen an audience this big. Usually it was tough to get their own parents to suffer through their twice-yearly concerts in the high-school auditorium.

But the applause was loud, and even though the band wasn't ever going to amount to much, Tamsin Milner had a voice on her. The soprano was no stranger to the people of Spruce Bay. She often sang at weddings and birthday parties and her sweet voice had coaxed more than one sinner into the Spruce Bay Baptist church on a Sunday morning.

Baseball caps came off and everyone stood silently and

respectfully as Tamsin sang the anthem, accompanied—not very well—by the band.

When the applause had died down, Ted's voice boomed, "And now, our referee, Ms. Lynette Lundstrom."

"She's not exactly impartial," somebody yelled.

"You keep your mouth shut, Bruce Parker, or I'll bang one of those hockey sticks over your head," yelled back Jerry Hodgkins, who then sipped something out of a silver flask.

"All righty, let's get this game under way."

And then, to her utter shock, a couple of high-school boys carried some kind of electronic equipment onto the ice.

"I'm sure many of you were wondering how these two people could play a decent game of hockey with only two of them." Ted Lowenbrau chuckled, a big hah, hah, hah that half the audience seemed to enjoy so much they joined in.

"We solved the problem by providing them with ready-made teams. In fact, Claire and Max will be backed up by their choice of NHL teams. They'll be playing Wii hockey."

Claire dropped her stick. She didn't mean to, but her fingers went slack.

She turned to Lynette, who seemed to be trying to hold back a grin. "Did you know about this?"

"They got my permission."

"But I've never played Wii hockey."

"I know. Max says he never has, either."

She snorted. "And you trust him?" She glared at him. He'd probably invented the game.

Lynette came forward, walking carefully on the slick surface. "Why don't you have fun with this? The only man I can think of who'd have made a gesture this romantic is your grandfather. I bet he's laughing himself silly right now."

Ted continued while the tech kids set up. "Now, neither of these players have ever played Wii hockey before, so they each get a personal coach to help them with the game. Ladies and gentlemen, please welcome Guillaume and Leo to the ice." The clapping intensified when two young boys came out wearing jeans, colorful sneakers and T-shirts with their favorite NHL teams on them.

"The boys are nine years old and they are both experts at the game. I know because one of them's my son and he pretty much only stops playing to go to school and to eat."

"Hi, Dad," one of the boys called out, waving.

Claire and Max had to stand side by side to play the game. When he approached, his eyes were so dark, so serious and sexy that she had to glance away. Why did she have to be in love with him? Why was she even here? This was the most ridiculous thing she'd ever done.

She glanced at the packed arena and couldn't help but recall all the times she'd played on this very ice in front of these very people. Her competitive instinct fired in spite of the absurdity of the situation.

"What were you thinking?" she whispered to her opponent.

"I wanted to sweep you off your feet."

She was genuinely shocked. "By making me play a video game in front of the whole town?"

He shrugged. "I'm a work in progress."

One of the boys handed her a controller that was shaped like a short hockey stick. Her coach, Guillaume, explained how the buttons on the controller worked. There was one to move the player, one to pass the puck and it seemed that by shaking the stick she could body-check her opponents. To shoot, she would swing the Wii hockey stick.

The game was broadcast on huge TV screens around the rink. Everybody seemed to be having a wonderful time, except for her.

The boys had picked their favorite NHL teams and she found herself concentrating on a TV screen. It was pretty amazing, she thought. The players looked almost real, the boards of the rink were covered in advertising and even the seats were full of supposed spectators.

"Okay," Guillaume said to her, as they prepared for their first face-off. "Hit the button a lot to try and get control of the puck."

The puck dropped. It was tumbling midair, about to strike ice when a terrible scream tore through the auditorium. "Oh, my God," a woman yelled. "The baby's coming."

The puck smacked the ice and neither she nor Max remembered to push the buttons.

Claire and Max both turned to where Jamie-Lynn was doubled over, being helped to her feet by her husband. Doc Bouton was standing by to take her other arm. The woman turned to the ice and yelled, "If it's a girl I'm calling it Claire. If it's a boy, it'll be Max."

Naturally, Claire turned to Max and found him looking at her with the sweetest expression a man can have while wearing a hockey jersey and holding a fake hockey stick. She started to melt, then remembered he was here to steal her company.

Lynette waited until Jamie-Lynn Burton, followed reluctantly by her husband and doctor, left the rink, and the yells of good wishes had died down. Then Lynette blew her whistle.

Game on.

She took Guillaume's advice and pushed the button a lot. Seemed she had control of the puck, but when she tried to pass it, the thing bounced up in the air and hit the boards. Her ineptitude was magnified on huge screens around the rink.

Max wasn't much better. He fumbled with his stick and there was chaos on the ice. The fake referee gave Max's team an icing call.

At the end of the first period, the score was zero-all. Lynette came over and patted Claire on the back.

"I suck at this."

"I know. So does Max. Don't worry, honey, people haven't had this much fun since that church group announced they were showing a film about the evils of alcohol at the civic auditorium. Do you remember that? It was *The Hangover*. Of course, nobody had the heart to tell them what kind of movie it was ahead of time. Mercy, that was funny."

But Claire wasn't interested in being the butt of a town joke. She was determined to take the game seriously, even if Max thought this whole thing was just for laughs.

She was starting to get the hang of the short stick with the buttons on it and there was an audience to entertain after all.

When the second period began she came on strong—after a little feinting and a few incredibly feeble attempts on his part to grab the puck from her, she acceded to the advice being yelled from the stands. "Show him what you're made of, Claire. Put that sucker in the net!"

She imagined that was her out there on the ice as she manipulated buttons and stick. She could picture Max's stunned expression as she roared past him, sprinting toward the net. She could hear her skates scratching ice, the roar of the crowd, her own breath huffing in and out as she pushed forward toward the empty net.

She stopped with a flourish, sending a spurt of ice scrapings into the air, and took a fraction of a second to set up her shot. Then she did what she'd been doing since she'd first seen the newspaper ad. She pictured Max's face on the puck and she smacked the black disk with all her strength, sending it flying, bang, into the net.

Somehow, her visualization got through to her hands and the remote thingy. Her little person on the screen scored.

The crowd went wild.

Actually wild. There was stomping, hollering, people got on their seats and jumped up and down, flasks were passed. Money changed hands. She hoped the Spruce Bay police force was ready for any fisticuffs that might break out.

"You go!"

And suddenly the sound system blasted out with the Vixens' theme song. "We Will Rock You" by Queen.

And then, when that died down, an enterprising member of the high-school band did a quick riff on his trumpet. More enthusiastic than musical, but she appreciated the sentiment.

The scoreboard lit up, flashing. Home Team: 1. Visitors: 0.

In case anyone had missed what had just happened, Ted got onto his mic. "Ladies and gentlemen, the first goal of the evening goes to Claire Lundstrom and Polar Air."

Claire took a moment to wave to the crowd—there was plenty of cheering and hollering and clapping to acknowledge.

Lynette blew her whistle. They were back with their fake sticks playing fake hockey. This time, Max grabbed the puck as soon as it touched the ice. He narrowed his gaze and for a second she saw the man who'd lost his chance at becoming an astronaut only to turn defeat into an amazing success. He hadn't become a whining sad sack. He'd turned his incredible brain and talent to what he could do. And he'd built an amazingly successful business.

Mr. Fumblefingers seemed to have figured out his controller.

His little player bullied his way past hers, checking her, so a big blast of yellow blossomed around her player like something out of a comic book. Max's team deftly maneuvered the puck while she stumbled in her attempt to bodycheck him.

She pushed buttons, darted around him, got in front of the puck.

His player deked around her.

Damn, that man was fast and smooth. Which shouldn't have surprised her.

She knew he was going to go left. It was his stronger side as a player so it made sense that would be his instinct even in a video game. She plunged left to check him and steal the puck.

He deked her out and went right.

While she raced to catch him she knew she was too late. Like her, Max kept his head under pressure. He took the moment to set up his shot even as she barreled down on him. Just as her player reached him he sent the puck flying into the net. "Great shot," she said, in spite of herself.

"Thanks. This is surprisingly tough."

He had a few fans. There was a bit of applause. His two friends from out of town did their best to create a cheering section, but they could only do so much.

Ted made the announcement and the scoreboard changed. Home: 1. Visitors: 1.

The game continued. If the stakes hadn't been so high she'd be having a blast. Who knew video-game hockey could be so much fun? Then, she'd suddenly remember that this wasn't a fun challenge.

It was serious.

The man with the sexy brown eyes and the dexterous hands was trying to take away her family's business.

After that the game turned into an intense battle as two motivated people tried to gain the upper hand with their beginner playing skills.

The second period ended, 1–1.

Both were sweating and exhausted by the time the whistle blew. She was almost as tired as she'd be if she were playing a real game of hockey.

And Max was playing to win.

While they took a short break, she visualized success, using every psychological trick she knew. She was interrupted by Laurel who'd come down to the ice to talk to her. Her friend sported glowing cheeks and a big smile.

"You are doing great," Laurel said.

"Thanks. I hope you've got the words of wisdom that will send me out there like a champ."

"Oh," Laurel said with a wave of her hand, "I know you'll win. You've got the hometown advantage."

"I hope it helps. I will never forgive Max for making such a fool of me. Of both of us."

"I met the chef!"

Since Claire still had her head in the game it took her a minute to respond. "What chef?"

"Felix Gerard! That chef. The one from the wilderness inn where you and Max stayed."

"Oh, right." She remembered now that she'd seen him.

"I decided to take the plunge. If I sit around being a polite wallflower all my life I'll end up a sad, toothless old woman still running the Spruce Bay Inn."

In spite of her inner heartache Claire had to smile. "I'm sure you'll still have your teeth."

"You know what I mean. Anyway, when I saw Max putting himself out like that for you, I figured, what the hell? During the break after first period I walked right up to him and introduced myself." She put a hand to her chest. "Those eyes. That accent. I'm already in love."

"Does he feel the same way?"

Her head bobbed back and forth. "Not sure. I think he's interested. He told me he's staying at the inn, so I'll have a chance to get to know him better."

"That's fantastic. Really."

You just never knew, Claire mused after Laurel left. Attraction, romance, love, the whole thing was such a mystery. She'd dated a reasonable number of men over the years. What made Max so special?

Why him of all men?

Even though she was angry and upset with him, even though he'd come to Spruce Bay under false pretenses to take over their company, she still couldn't deny the pull of attraction.

They were opponents on the ice and she wanted to pull off all his clothes and take him, right there on the rink.

She needed her head examined.

She was called back to the game. Third period. Score tied.

Time to wrap this up and send Max home with his tail between his legs.

When she came back onto the ice she sensed that the crowd was expecting her to do just that. They knew her, had rooted for her for years. Max was an outsider. A usurper. Nobody wanted him to win.

Feed on that, she told herself. Home-ice advantage, as Laurel had reminded her, was powerful stuff.

Her young coach said, "Hit the button a lot, try and get the puck." Claire nodded. She was a woman with a mission and no man, no matter how sexy he was, was going to sidetrack her. She was going to win this ridiculous game.

She flexed her fingers. Got herself into position, trying not to think about how ridiculous she must look in her hockey uniform and skates playing a video game with a short black plastic stick with buttons on it. Took the puck off him and—damn, he had it back before she'd got halfway to his net.

The battle continued. Neither one gave the other any openings. She'd pulled out her A game. Now she was reaching for an A+ game and hoping she actually had one.

Now that they were getting pretty good, the game was becoming more interesting.

She had her center forward pass to the left wing and back to center. When Max accidentally sent his defense in the wrong direction, the puck slid neatly into his net. 2–1.

Okay, she told herself. All she had to do was play defense from now on. Keep his shots out of her net and she'd win.

Easy peasy.

But Max had other ideas.

And, with a minute to go in regular time, he shot left when she guessed he'd go right. And tied the game up.

She was so tired and frustrated she wanted to throw something.

What were they going to do now? Sudden death?

A shoot-out?

"Cool," said Leo. "You guys are doing okay for beginners."

"Thanks."

She wanted this to be over. She wanted to take her airline and go home. She wasn't the only one who felt that way. There were groans from the audience. A bit of bad-natured booing, but she understood where it was coming from. She felt like booing herself. Or boohooing.

The announcer came on.

"Ladies and gentlemen, the score is tied. And what an exciting game it's been." He paused for the applause. "Now, we're going to give these players a short break and then come back for sudden-death overtime."

"No."

She glanced up and found it was Max who had said the word. Loud and clear. "No."

He skated toward the announcer and gestured for the mic. With a shrug, Ted handed it to him.

"As you all know, I came here today to challenge Claire Lundstrom to a game. My company wants to buy Polar Air. Claire doesn't want to talk to me."

There was mostly dead silence with a couple of rude comments thrown in.

"Now, you people don't know me or my company but we're not corporate raiders." He paused to wipe a bead of sweat from his temple. "We can shoot it out in sudden-death overtime and decide whether Claire's going to hear my proposal or whether I'm going to go away. But it seems like there might be another option."

"Like what?"

Claire had been so busy listening to Max that she hadn't noticed Lynette come back onto the ice and stalk up to where Max was standing.

Max turned to the older woman, but he kept talking into the microphone so everyone could hear him. "I've never offered this before, but I might consider a partnership. Instead of my company taking over and buying you out, we could negotiate a partnership arrangement. Details to be worked out later."

"It's not just a business to us," Lynette informed him, her voice so loud she didn't need a mic. "It's our home."

"I know. And you will have your home. We'll exclude it from the deal. Your house and your part of the waterfront are yours to keep."

"Take the deal, Lynette!" somebody yelled.

But Lynette wasn't finished with Max yet. She glanced back at Claire who felt as though she was frozen into the rink. She couldn't seem to move.

"What about Claire? She needs a home, too."

He turned to Claire with an understanding smile. Her grandmother was really putting her on the spot. "I agree. I propose to give Claire a home for life. With me."

"What's that supposed to mean?" Lynette demanded. "You looking at one of those live-in arrangements? I don't approve of those. I think you should marry the girl."

"Lynette!" Claire could feel her cheeks begin to burn. She forced her skates to move forward.

"I agree," Max said. "I think I should marry the girl, too."

She'd have stamped her foot if it didn't currently have

a skate on it. Instead, she handed Guillaume her stick, then she whooshed up to where Max and Lynette had formed a cozy twosome on the ice.

"I am not marrying a man because my grandmother told him he has to."

This had to be the most embarrassing moment of her life. Her grandmother was bargaining to get her a husband in front of the entire town. She could hear snickers and whispering—she'd never live this day down as long as she lived.

Perhaps Max understood how she felt because he came forward. When he realized he was holding the mic, he handed it to Lynette.

He came closer, until they were almost touching. "I'm not asking because your grandmother wants me to. I'm asking because I love you and I want to spend the rest of my life with you."

"I—" She glanced around at all the eager faces staring at them. "Oh, this is ridiculous."

"I know. I really needed to get your attention and I wanted everyone to understand that I'm serious about this town, serious about you."

He dug into his shorts and to her shock brought out a jewelry box. She was no expert but she was pretty sure it was from Tiffany. He flipped it open and the flash of diamond beamed out at her. It was gorgeous. Big enough to make a statement but not "I'm richer than you are" show-offy big. "Oh, Max."

"I don't care whether we buy Polar Air or not. I only want you. Will you marry me?"

"Oh, Max."

"Kiss the girl, you fool!"

He chuckled softly. Reached forward and kissed her gently. She felt the passion and love as his lips brushed hers, then with a tiny murmur, she moved closer, and he pulled her to him so they were kissing and hugging and laughing.

"Yes. In order to save my business, I will marry you."

"You won't only be saving your business, you'll be saving me."

"Really?"

"I was restless and bored. I didn't know what I wanted to do with the rest of my life." He reached forward and took her left hand. "Now, I do." He took her ring finger and slipped the big, gorgeous ring onto it. "I want to spend every day with you. Lie by your side every night. Have children with you."

"Play hockey with me?"

He laughed. "Anytime you want."

"I love you."

And as they kissed and hugged each other, Lynette whispered to Ted. He grinned and nodded.

The scoreboard lit up.

It was a home-team win.

THERE WERE congratulations, hugs, a few tears from Lynette and even a couple from Claire herself. In the midst of it all, she became aware that the three strangers she'd noticed earlier were surrounding Max, arm-punching and shoving and generally acting like fools. The three men, Max and two taller guys, were pretty much a trio of gorgeous. The woman was gazing at them with calm amusement but Claire could see how her eyes lit when they rested on the tallest of the three. She suspected her own eyes did the same when she looked at Max.

"Claire," her brand-new fiancé called out, looking so happy her heart melted all over again. "Come on over and meet my best friends."

She did. "Ladies first," Max said. "Claire Lundstrom, this is Serena Long."

The women shook hands, then Serena said, "You know we're going to be spending a lot of time together in the future." And she pulled Claire in for a hug. In a low voice, she said, "I've known Max for a long time and I've never seen him look so happy. Thank you."

"He makes me happy, too," she said, still amazed that the man she'd tried to despise only a few hours ago was going to be her husband.

"Serena's going to marry Adam, here," Max said, continuing the introductions.

The tallest of the three opened his mouth but was forestalled by Gorgeous #2 who said, "Hey, you guys should have a double wedding."

"And the mouthy guy is Dylan."

Dylan's grin was the kind that could get a girl in trouble, Claire thought. And she bet he used it shamelessly. "Seriously," Dylan said. "When Max told us that you were a hockey-playing bush pilot, I might have had some doubts about my old buddy's taste in girls." He looked her up and down and said, "But you are about the prettiest hockey-playing bush pilot I've ever seen."

"Trust me," Max said, putting an arm around her. "He means that as a compliment."

She accepted Dylan's hug. Then Adam came forward. "I'm looking forward to getting to know you. But I think Max finally got it right."

The two couples stood close. Max reached for Claire's hand and she realized that Adam and Serena were also holding hands.

She glanced at Dylan, hoping he didn't feel left out, and caught him looking at the two couples. For just a second she thought she saw a wistful expression cross his face and then he suddenly stuck both fists in the air and did a kind of victory dance. "And I guess that makes me the Last Bachelor Standing!"

Max was still holding his hockey-stick-shaped controller in his free hand. "Here." He offered it to Dylan. "Play on."

In seconds, Dylan was huddled with Guillaume and Leo learning the finer points of Wii hockey.

Adam and Max exchanged glances. "Think he'll ever grow up?" Adam asked.

Max replied, "All he needs is the love of the right woman. It's amazing what love can do." And he leaned over and kissed Claire.

As she threw her arms around him and kissed him back, she realized he was right. It was amazing what love could do.

* * * * *

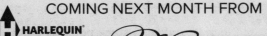

REQUEST YOUR FREE BOOKS!
2 FREE NOVELS PLUS 2 FREE GIFTS!

red-hot reads!

YES! Please send me 2 FREE Harlequin® Blaze™ novels and my 2 FREE gifts (gifts are worth about $10). After receiving them, if I don't wish to receive any more books, I can return the shipping statement marked "cancel." If I don't cancel, I will receive 4 brand-new novels every month and be billed just $4.74 per book in the U.S. or $4.96 per book in Canada. That's a savings of at least 14% off the cover price. It's quite a bargain. Shipping and handling is just 50¢ per book in the U.S. and 75¢ per book in Canada.* I understand that accepting the 2 free books and gifts places me under no obligation to buy anything. I can always return a shipment and cancel at any time. Even if I never buy another book, the two free books and gifts are mine to keep forever.

150/350 HDN F4WC

Name	(PLEASE PRINT)

Address	Apt. #

City	State/Prov.	Zip/Postal Code

Signature (if under 18, a parent or guardian must sign)

Mail to the **Harlequin® Reader Service:**
IN U.S.A.: P.O. Box 1867, Buffalo, NY 14240-1867
IN CANADA: P.O. Box 609, Fort Erie, Ontario L2A 5X3

Want to try two free books from another line?
Call 1-800-873-8635 or visit www.ReaderService.com.

* Terms and prices subject to change without notice. Prices do not include applicable taxes. Sales tax applicable in N.Y. Canadian residents will be charged applicable taxes. Offer not valid in Quebec. This offer is limited to one order per household. Not valid for current subscribers to Harlequin Blaze books. All orders subject to credit approval. Credit or debit balances in a customer's account(s) may be offset by any other outstanding balance owed by or to the customer. Please allow 4 to 6 weeks for delivery. Offer available while quantities last.

Your Privacy—The Harlequin® Reader Service is committed to protecting your privacy. Our Privacy Policy is available online at www.ReaderService.com or upon request from the Harlequin Reader Service.

We make a portion of our mailing list available to reputable third parties that offer products we believe may interest you. If you prefer that we not exchange your name with third parties, or if you wish to clarify or modify your communication preferences, please visit us at www.ReaderService.com/consumerschoice or write to us at Harlequin Reader Service Preference Service, P.O. Box 9062, Buffalo, NY 14269. Include your complete name and address.

HB13R2

SPECIAL EXCERPT FROM

 HARLEQUIN®

 *Blaze*®

Bestselling author Leslie Kelly brings you a
sizzling sneak peak of the latest **Unrated!** story
from Harlequin® Blaze®!

Double Take

Available May 2014 wherever
Harlequin books are sold.

Suddenly the ferry lurched again, making him glad for his
strong grip on the railing. But the woman—Lindsey—wobbled
on her feet and, for a second, he thought she'd fall. Not even
thinking about it, he stepped into her path and grabbed her
before she could stumble.

Their legs tangled, hips bumped and chests collided. He
had a chance to suck in a shocked—and pleased—breath,
when her fine red hair whipped across his face, bringing with
it a flowery fragrance that cut through the briny air and went
right to his head. Just like this woman was doing.

"Whoa," she murmured, either because of the stumbling
or the fact that so much of her was now touching so much
of him.

"I've got you," he said, placing a firm hand on her shoulder. He turned his back to the wind, staying close, but giving
her some distance and disengaging the more vulnerable parts
of their bodies. As nice as she had felt pressed against him, he
didn't want her to know that his lower half was ignoring his
brain's order to be a polite protector and was instead going

straight for horny man. Their new position removed the danger of sensual overload, but also kept her blocked from the worst of the wind. "I won't let you fall overboard. Now glove up."

Not taking no for an answer, he lifted one of her small, cold hands and shoved a glove on it. He forced himself to focus only on the fact that her lips now had a bluish tint, not that they were pretty damned kissable. And that her expression was pure misery, not that her face was shaped like a perfect heart, with high cheekbones and a pointy, stubborn little chin.

Once her hands were adequately protected, she stepped the tiniest bit closer, as if welcoming the shelter of his body. Mike heaved in a deep breath of cold lake air, but found it tasted of spicy-fragranced woman.

Nice. Very nice.

She licked her lips. "So you're single, too?"

He noticed she didn't add *available*, maybe because she didn't want to sound like she was interested, though he could tell she was; but he recognized desire when he saw it. During those few moments when she'd landed hard against him, heat had flared between them, instinctive and powerful.

"I'm *very* single."

This unexpected hunk might be just what she needs!

According to his trading card, steady, marriage-minded—and gorgeous!—Max Dorset sounds tailor-made for Natalie Gellar. But when they meet, she realizes Max is only interested in a good time with no strings attached!

Don't miss the latest in the *It's Trading Men!* miniseries,

Seduce Me
by *Jo Leigh*

Available May 2014 wherever you buy Harlequin Blaze books.

Available now from the
It's Trading Men! miniseries by Jo Leigh:

Choose Me
Want Me
Have Me

HARLEQUIN®

Blaze®

Red-Hot Reads
www.Harlequin.com

HB79800